SAMMY
joins the
shooting stars

SAMMY
joins the shooting stars

michele cox

■ HarperCollins*Publishers*

National Library of New Zealand Cataloguing-in-Publication Data
Cox, Michele, 1968-
Sammy joins the shooting stars / Michele Cox.
ISBN 978-1-86950-741-1
[1. Soccer—Fiction.] I. Title.
NZ823.3—dc 22

First published 2008
HarperCollins*Publishers (New Zealand) Limited*
P.O. Box 1, Auckland

ISBN 978 1 86950 741 1

Cover and internal illustrations by Scott Tulloch
Cover design by Matt Stanton and Alicia Freile
Typesetting by Springfield West

Printed by Griffin Press, Australia

50gsm Bulky News used by HarperCollins*Publishers* is a natural,
recyclable product made from wood grown in sustainable
plantation forests. The manufacturing processes conform to the
environmental regulations in the country of origin, New Zealand.

This is for my own mum, dad, and Coach Kev. And for those just like them, who believe that girls really can play.

Foreword

A while ago I said the future of football is feminine. Indeed, the future of football is millions of little girls like Sammy all around the world, bringing more joy, skill and passion to the game. I hope that you enjoy Sammy's journey into the football family, and that she inspires you to take up your own path into the beautiful game.

Joseph S. Blatter
FIFA President

Sammy jumped over the poppies onto the grass of the playing field. She looked down at her new Comet shoes as they touched the grass for the first time. Her shaggy black hair fell all over her face. The ponytail on the top of her head drooped forward and tickled her nose, so she blew hard at it and shook her head. The snork, which is what she called it, flipped back.

'One small step for girlkind,' she giggled to her dog, Splodge, 'and one step for my new Comet shoes.'

Sammy wriggled her feet in the shoes. The grass felt spongy beneath them. Then she glided in crazy slow motion, like an astronaut, onto the football pitch. Splodge stood and watched her, cocking his head to one side.

As she moon-walked slowly into the centre of the pitch, all the time looking down at her shoes, her ponytail flipped back over her face. Splodge barked and Sammy quickly looked up. An older girl, Renee, was putting her football shoes on at the other end of the field. When she heard Splodge bark, Renee looked over at them and waved.

Renee was a much more experienced football player than Sammy. Of course she'd be up here, on the field, practising at the weekend.

'Just trying out my shoes,' Sammy shouted an explanation. Renee did some warm-up stretches then walked across the field towards Sammy and Splodge.

'Hi, Splodge,' she said. 'Hi, Sammy. Why don't you start breaking those shoes in with some dribbling practice? I could run with the ball at my feet and you could try to get it off me. I can try tricks and turns to stop you taking it away, though.'

'OK,' said Sammy. 'But I'm not very good at it.'

'All the more reason to practise,' said Renee with a smile.

The two girls practised dribbling together. They started off up the field, but Splodge decided it was a game for three. He kept darting in and trying to take the ball away.

'Sorry, Renee. He's not the best practice mate.'

'I'm going to run around the field for a while,' Renee said. 'Keep dribbling. Two minutes up, then two minutes back.'

Splodge gave three woofs. Sammy told him, sternly, 'It's hard work. I'll start, then you can have your turn. OK, let's go.'

Sammy rolled the ball away from Splodge and ran after it. When she started dribbling the ball, Splodge was right on her heels. 'And you have to be fair. No grabbing hold of my socks or shorts. No cheating!'

He followed her every move. They went all over the field. Up and down, and side to side.

All the time, Sammy was trying to keep her body between Splodge and the ball. Splodge, on the other hand, was trying to get his nose on the ball. He tried three times to run around the outside to get the ball off Sammy. He wanted to dodge in front and nip the ball away from Sammy. Each time she chopped the ball back on the inside so he couldn't.

However, Splodge was a very clever dog. He tricked Sammy by pretending to run down the outside again. When Sammy went to move the ball inside, he darted through her legs. Straight into the ball he went with his nose. Sammy got more and more frustrated. She looked up. Renee was standing, hands on hips, watching.

Sammy felt embarrassed.

'He knows how to play football,' Renee laughed. 'Your mistake, Sammy, was doing that trick too many times.'

'Did I? But if it was a good trick—'

'No. You have to outwit your opponent *all* the time. Splodge knew what you were going to do, didn't you, Splodge?'

Splodge didn't answer. He just stood, legs far apart, head down. His eyes never left the ball.

'So Splodge planned a move to take it off me,' said Sammy.

'OK, I get it. What can I do to make sure he doesn't do that to me again? I know . . .'

Sammy set off for another go. This time, she did different things. Renee stood still and watched. Sammy went straight, sideways, made number eight patterns on the grass and all sorts of other moves. She moved the ball in front, from the inside to the outside, and from outside to in. Splodge had no idea what she was going to do next. He couldn't get the ball. And suddenly the two minutes were up.

'Yay,' said Sammy. 'I made it!'

Renee shouted from down the field, 'Good one!' Sammy waved back to her and Splodge waved his tail. Sammy bent down to put her face near his nose.

'You didn't get the ball. I wouldn't let you get it. I won. But it's your turn now. Let's see if I can get it off you. Ready, steady, go.'

Splodge put his nose down. Nudging the ball, he zoomed off. He zipped here and there, all the time keeping the ball at the edge of his nose. Sammy had to run like mad to keep up with him. She was really puffed, but she kept going.

Renee yelled: 'Keep your eye on the ball!'

Sammy looked up and over to Renee.

'Not on me, the ball!' Renee shouted.

Sammy concentrated on the ball, and chased after Splodge. Most importantly, she watched what Splodge was doing.

Splodge's two minutes were nearly up. Sammy hadn't got the ball once. Sammy lay down on the field, panting.

'I can't get it off him,' she said to Renee, who walked over slowly. 'I don't think I'm any good at football.'

'No one's good at anything if they don't put in the effort,' Renee said.

Sammy shook her hair. 'No. I can't get the hang of it.'

'You can.'

'How?'

'You have to out-think him.'

'Out-thinking a dog might be hard,' smiled Sammy. 'Anyway, I've had enough of this. Football's not my thing.'

From what Renee had just seen, she thought Sammy could play football. 'No,' said Renee. 'Keep at it. Do it again with Splodge. Get it off him this time. Bet you can.'

Renee set the timer on her watch for another two minutes. 'Go!' she yelled.

Splodge bounced about on four stiff legs, then shot off with the ball. Sammy chased him. Then she noticed something. After Splodge zigged, he always zagged. So the very next time he went left, she stepped forward to the right.

When Splodge turned to go right, the ball ran straight into Sammy's feet.

'One-all,' yelled Sammy. 'It's a draw.'

The two of them collapsed on the grass. Even Splodge was puffed this time. His tongue was hanging out and he was panting. When Sammy got her breath back, she said to him, 'It was hard work eh, Splodge? But it was so much fun. I liked it a lot.'

'You liked it because you out-thought him,' said Renee, running over to them.

'Did I?' Sammy felt pleased with herself. 'What shall we do now?' she asked Renee. 'You're a good football player. Can you do one of those flick tricks? Show me. I can try and copy you.'

Sammy watched closely. Renee was the best girl football player Sammy knew. When she was Sammy's age, Renee had been in the Shooting Stars team. And Sammy knew you had to be excellent to be in the Shooting Stars.

Sammy had seen Renee on the field before, doing flicks with the ball.

'OK. Watch this!' said Renee, neatly flicking the ball

behind her with her foot, and the ball curved up in the air and landed in front of her.

After Renee did her flick trick the fifth time, Sammy told her, 'I think I know how to do it now. Let me have a go.'

Sammy went over to the ball and put her feet tightly around it.

All I have to do is flick it behind me and up over my head, she thought. *How hard can that be?*

She counted to three. On three, she flicked her legs up behind her. When her legs had gone as far as they could, she let go of the ball. The ball, however, didn't go up over her head. It went straight up and hit her in the bum.

'Ow ahh,' Sammy said as she rubbed her bum. 'I think I let it go too late.'

Renee laughed, but it wasn't a mean laugh. She picked up the ball and handed it back to Sammy. Sammy tried again, making sure she let it go earlier. This time, though, it was a little bit too early. The ball went shooting out behind her, nearly flying into Splodge. Luckily he ducked. The ball went sailing over the top of him.

'Sorry, I wasn't aiming for you. Honest,' Sammy said as she ran to get the ball.

Over and over again she tried to do the trick. Each time the ball hit her on the bum, back or head. Or it flew off in a different direction. It didn't hurt, but it was really frustrating.

Twenty times she tried. It had looked so easy when Renee did it.

'Renee!' Someone was calling across the field.

'Coming!' It was Renee's mother, come to pick her up. 'Gotta go, Sammy.'

Renee ran.

'Bye, and thanks,' shouted Sammy.

When Renee was on the other side of the field she yelled, 'Keep practising! You'll be good!' then she turned and disappeared down the hill.

Sammy was alone on the field now, and it was getting late. It was nearly time for dinner. But Sammy had a mission. She just had to get this flick right.

Finally, on the 21st time, the ball flicked up perfectly. It went over her head and bounced on the ground in front of where she was standing.

'Did you see that? I did it. Yay! I thought it was going to be easy, but it was much harder than I thought. I've got it sussed now, though — it's done and dusted. Shall we do some kicking before we go home?' Sammy asked.

Playing fetch was Splodge's favourite game. He loved running after Sammy's kicks. He ran down the field towards the apartment buildings opposite the brick clubhouse. When he was 15 metres away from Sammy, he stopped and turned around. Whenever she had tried kicking the ball before, 15 metres was the furthest she'd ever managed.

Splodge woofed to tell Sammy he was ready. Sammy took five steps back from the ball. She took a good run up and put her non-kicking foot beside the ball. Her other foot swung underneath. It felt really good when she connected. The ball flew. And flew. And flew. And kept flying.

The ball was meant to stop in front of Splodge. It went over his head. Way over his head. It also went way over the poppies at the edge of the field. It went up, up, up, then curved. It started coming down.

'No!' yelled Sammy. She could see what was going to happen. The ball, still travelling fast, was headed straight for one of the apartments. And, oh no, no, the apartment the ball was headed for had a large window. And that window was wide open.

'No!'

Along with the rest of the town of Eden, Sammy knew that this was where Coach Kev lived. He was really famous, and coached the town's best football team, the Shooting Stars. Last year the team had won the junior national club title. They were in the paper and on the TV. Everyone in Eden was very proud of them, knew who all the players were, and everyone knew Coach Kev.

Coach Kev picked and trained the boys and girls in the Shooting Stars, and he knew just about everything about football. He could tell you all the names of the famous players, like Beckham, Ronaldo, Marta and Prinz. He could even tell you what they were and weren't good at. The same went for his own team. Coach Kev knew exactly what his players needed to do to get better, and he made sure they did. Otherwise Coach Kev wasn't happy. When the players didn't try to improve and play better or do what he said, he could be more than just unhappy. He could be scary.

When the ball flew through the window of his apartment, Coach Kev was just sitting down to afternoon tea. That morning he had trained hard and gone for a long run, so he was allowing himself a treat. His absolute favourite food was warm custard and ice cream. At exactly the same moment as Sammy kicked the ball, he was bending over a huge bowl of warm custard and vanilla ice cream.

The table he was sitting at was by the window. The bowl was in front of him. He was just about to dip his spoon into the yummy custard, when SPLOSH! Sammy's ball came flying through the window, landing smack in the middle of his custard. The ice cream was well and truly squashed, but the warm yellow custard splattered all over Coach Kev. It was in his hair, on his face, and even in his ears. Coach Kev's nice white shirt now had star-like splotches on it. He was not happy.

Coach Kev knew the ball had come through the window. Someone on the field must have kicked it at him. 'Who splashed me with custard?' he yelled out at the top of his voice. 'Grrrrrrr-glurgh!'

The grrrrrrr turned into a bit of a gurgle as some custard dripped off the end of his nose and into his mouth.

Down on the field, Sammy looked at Splodge.

Uh oh, she thought. *I've really done it now! He's going to be so mad at me.*

She stood there, unable to move. Coach Kev stuck his head out of the window. Custard was dripping down his nose onto the poppies below. He looked at her, then at Splodge. Then he looked around the field. Coach Kev seemed confused. He was looking for someone, and it wasn't Sammy. But there was no one else there.

'Where's the player who kicked that ball?' he roared.

Sammy just stood there, not moving, not talking.

He looked around the field again. No, there was no one else there.

'Did *you* kick this ball?' he asked, finally.

Sammy nodded. 'I'm very sorry,' she said. 'I didn't mean it to go so far.' She put her head down in shame.

'Hrrrrmp,' spluttered the coach. Then he asked, less angrily, 'Did you kick it from where you're standing?'

'Yes.' Her voice came out in a tiny tremble.

'Hmm. What's your name?'

'I'm Sammy Banks and this is my dog Splodge. I live—'

'Sammy Banks, eh?'

'Are you going to tell my father?'

'Oooh, maybe I'll leave that for you to do.'

'Am I in trouble, Coach Kev?'

The coach peered down from the windowsill, looked around the field one more time, then said: 'Wait there, Sammy Banks. I'll bring your ball back. I'd also like to talk to you about what you just did.'

Oh no, thought Sammy. *Something bad is going to happen — I'm really in trouble now.* She dug a little hole in the grass with her new shoes as she stood there waiting miserably. Scared and ashamed, she didn't know what the coach was about to do. Her mind whirled around. First, she thought about her parents. *What am I going to tell Mum and Dad? They'll be really mad and won't let me come up here again. They'll probably take away my new football shoes. Maybe they won't let me take Splodge for walks again. Maybe I'll be grounded.*

Then she began to feel that it just wasn't fair. *But I really didn't know the ball would go that far. How could I have known? It just took off. It was something to do with the way I kicked it.*

Then her thoughts changed to plans for escape. *What if I just take off right now? He won't catch me. I didn't tell him where I live.* She thought about it a bit more. Her mum and dad would be even angrier if she ran away. They would say she was being irresponsible.

Finally, she shook her head. No. That was what a coward would do. Maybe, if she explained what had happened, her parents would understand. She hadn't meant to, after all. It was an accident.

She knew she wasn't going to run away. Sammy called Splodge over next to her and folded her arms. By now Coach Kev was walking across the field. Her heart was thumping.

Please don't let him be too angry, she prayed.

It felt like forever before Coach Kev reached her, although it only really took a few minutes. When he arrived, he slowly put the custard-smeared ball down on the ground. Then he wiped his hand on the grass, before he put his hand out to Sammy and said, 'My name is Coach Kev. I'm the coach of the Shooting Stars.'

'Er — I know,' she said.

Sammy shook his hand and put her head straight back down again. Her snork hung beside her ear.

'Have you heard of them, Sammy?'

She didn't want to look at him in case she cried.

'Yes, Coach Kev,' Sammy replied. She was holding her breath, waiting to be told off.

'Tell me what happened,' he said.

She looked up and saw he was still dripping with custard.

She was so surprised, she started to smile. Smiling at his dripping face wasn't a good idea, but she couldn't stop. It made her feel better. She took a deep breath.

'I wanted to try out my new Comet shoes and I was practising my kicking. Before, I could only kick 15 metres, so I thought it would only go to where Splodge was waiting. But when I kicked the ball, it just kept going up and up. I'm really sorry, Coach Kev. I really didn't think it would go so far. I didn't mean it, especially not for it to go through your window. Or—' she stopped, and looked at his yellow chin again, 'to splash you with custard.'

Splodge started licking the custard off Coach Kev's shoes. Sammy was horrified. 'Stop that, Splodge,' she said and yanked him away. *Now I'm really done for*, she thought.

Sammy needn't have worried. 'It's OK,' Coach Kev laughed. 'He's helping clean my shoes. It's also OK about the ball landing in my custard. I can see you're sorry and that you didn't mean it. I think next time you'll be a bit more careful. Will you promise me that?'

'Of course, Coach Kev. I'm totally sorry. Next time I'll make sure I play well away from the apartments,' she answered. Her voice was still a bit shaky, but she was very relieved that she was not in more trouble.

'You don't play for a football team, do you?'

'No. I just kick around with Splodge up here at the park.'

'I thought I hadn't seen you at any of the games. What I would like you to do is think carefully about something for me.'

Sammy looked up at him and nodded.

'I'd like you to think about coming down to train with my Shooting Stars next week after school. They have their last training session before the start of the season. If I think you're good enough and you like it, you can join the team.'

Sammy was stunned. 'But they're the best team — they're national champions!' she gasped.

'Sure they are, Sammy. But if you can kick far enough for your ball to land in my custard, I think you may have some real talent. You could add something to the team. You'll have to work hard and catch up to the others; after all, they've been there a lot longer. They've also put in a lot of effort to be the best. If you have the right attitude, though, I think you can do it. We'll see soon enough. What do you think?'

Sammy was still shocked. Everyone wanted to play for the Shooting Stars. 'Yes, of course, I'd love to try out for the team.

That would be amazing,' she managed to say.

'OK, Sammy. That's great. Please go home and ask your parents to call me. They need to let me know that you're allowed to play. I can also tell them where and when you need to come to training. Here's my card, it has my phone number on it. See you next week, I hope,' he said. Then he turned and walked back to his apartment to make some more custard and ice cream.

'Wow, Splodge. What do you think of that! I can't believe it. Coach Kev wants me to try out for his team. And I thought he was going to tell me off. Let's go home and tell Mum and Dad the news,' she said as she picked up her ball.

Running across the field and then down the steps, Sammy felt very excited. She'd always wanted to join a football team. At night, she dreamed of being Marta. Marta was the best female player in the whole world. She played for Brazil and was famous for scoring beautiful goals. When she had the ball, Marta also dribbled around people as if they weren't even there. She was so fast and skillful. The crowds loved Marta and always cheered extra loudly when she was on the field. Sammy thought it would be fantastic to be just like her.

Suddenly Sammy stopped and sat down on one of the steps. She put her head between her knees and sighed. Splodge had no idea what was wrong, and went over to her and licked her ear.

'Ewww, Splodge. Gross.' Splodge was still worried, so he put his front right paw on her leg.

'You're worried about me, aren't you?' Sammy asked him.

'Woof.' He snuggled in closer to Sammy. She looked so sad. Two minutes ago she had been the happiest girl in the world.

'It's just that I'm not sure I can do it. The Shooting Stars are so good. They are the absolute best. I know all the rules and I've watched lots of games and I've played lots of times with you, but I've never played for a team. The others will be twenty times better than me. I won't know what to do and I don't want to let them down. And what if they're all boys?'

That was a scary thought.

Splodge grabbed hold of Sammy's shorts and started pulling her down the steps.

'What are you doing? You'll rip my shorts. Stop!' Sammy

protested. Splodge held on fast to Sammy's shorts with his teeth. He kept pulling her down the steps. He got her all the way to the bottom, before she told him he really had to stop right there and then.

Splodge let go of Sammy's shorts and they walked on until they reached the family's football-shaped letterbox. She reached up and pressed the red number 11 on the front. A letter flew out the top, just like toast popping out of the toaster. 'It's for Dad,' Sammy said as she read the writing on the front.

Sammy pulled a ripe orange off one of the fruit trees in their garden and began peeling it as they walked up the path. Her father's office was at the front of the house. Mr Banks was sitting at his desk working on the computer.

'Dad, I have a letter for you,' she said. 'Can I come in?'

'Of course, Sammy,' he replied. 'I see you're wearing your new shoes. Have you been up at the park testing them out? How were they?'

'Dad, they were great. Too great in fact,' Sammy said, looking down at them as she handed her father his letter, feeling her cheeks start to go pink with embarrassment.

'Are you OK? You don't look too good. And how can your shoes be too great?' he asked her.

'It's a long story, Dad.'

'Well, I have time before dinner for a long story. Come and sit down on the chair here and tell me.' He patted the big, comfy chair next to his desk and Sammy jumped up on it.

She started to speak, then stopped. Maybe she should just keep what had happened up at the park a secret. After all, Coach Kev said he wasn't going to tell anyone.

But her parents always seemed to find out anyway if she didn't tell them something. How, she didn't know. Not wanting to get into any more trouble, she decided to tell her dad everything. From the ball landing in Coach Kev's big bowl of custard to him asking her to try out for the Shooting Stars.

Sammy's dad listened to the whole story. He didn't say anything at all until she'd finished and given him Coach Kev's card.

'That's some story. First of all, you were very lucky that Coach Kev was so nice about it. He might not have been so understanding if his window had been closed. You might have been paying for a broken window. But I'm pleased you said sorry and didn't run away.

'I'm very proud that he asked you to try out for the Shooting Stars. That's a real honour, Sammy. Lots of young footballers dream about playing for them, and some of them practise for months and still don't get a chance. So why aren't you jumping up and down with a big smile on your face?'

'Dad, the Shooting Stars are the absolute best, and I've never even played for a team. What if I go to training and I don't know what to do? I might look really stupid.'

'Oh, Sammy. When you start something new, of course you're not going to be as good as the others. Yes, the others will have a head start, and you may never be as good as some of them. They are the best of the best, after all. But that doesn't mean that in time you won't be as good. Coach Kev knows that, and he won't expect you to be able to do everything the others can right away. What he will expect is that you listen to him and try hard to learn as much as you can. That's what he'll be looking for.'

'So, he won't expect me to do 100 juggles with the ball and things like that?'

'Not to start with, but he'll probably show you how. Coach Kev will ask you to practise so that you do get good at those things. It'll be a bit like homework, but a lot more fun.'

'Hmmm. I'm not sure, Dad.'

'How do you think you'll feel if you don't try out? You'll watch the Shooting Stars playing and always wonder if you could have been out there with them, running around, shooting goals, making new friends. All the good stuff. Doesn't that sound better than sitting and just watching? Especially sitting and watching, and thinking *I might have been able to do that*.

'You've always wanted to play football. Now is your chance. And what a chance it is! Think carefully about whether being a little bit scared is worth turning it down.'

'You're right, Dad. So you won't be mad at me if I go and Coach Kev doesn't pick me?'

'Of course not. I'd be more upset if you didn't give it a go. And do you know what? I think that, as long as you work hard at the training, you'll be fantastic. Plus you have two secret weapons to help you.'

'My secret weapons?' Sammy thought for a moment. 'Ah,' she said. 'My Comet shoes are definitely one. The ball goes really far when I kick with them.'

'That's right. When you put them on, you'll shine like the stars in the sky.'

Sammy didn't quite know what that meant. But she liked the sound of it.

'But you said two. What's my other secret weapon?'

'Your mind. If you're really smart, you can outplay other players who are better than you. If you get into the team, there will be players who will be much bigger and stronger. You need to spend time thinking about how you can use the things you are good at to help you.

'Start by believing in yourself. And that means believing that you can do something, even when it's really difficult. The more you see yourself doing something, the more it will happen. You'll see.'

'Like believing I'll be good at training next week?'

'Exactly. When you're in bed tonight, say *I believe, I do* 10 times. Then picture yourself scoring a great goal at training. Perhaps a huge kick that goes in the top corner of the net. One that makes Mum and me clap and cheer, and makes Coach Kev give you a big pat on the back. Do you think you can do that?'

'I think so,' said Sammy, nodding her head. 'So, does that mean you'll ring Coach Kev and tell him I can play?'

'I'll do that tonight. Would you like that?'

'Absolutely, Dad. Thanks so much.' She gave her father a hug and went to lay the table for dinner.

That night Sammy lay in bed in her favourite pyjamas. They looked more like Argentina's football strip than real pyjamas, and she just loved them. The top had light blue and white vertical stripes, and the bottoms were black. Best of all, the number 10 was written in white on the back, with her name SAMMY written above it. Number 10 was where she wanted to play. You could do everything in that position. Attack, defend, shoot, tackle, run, head the ball — everything except save the goals with your hands. That was the goal-keeper's job.

Sammy wanted so much to be a Shooting Star. *After all,* she thought, *a real shooting star shines really bright and zooms everywhere for all to see.*

As she lay in her bed, Sammy did what her father had told her to do before dinner. Although she felt a bit silly, she repeated 'I believe, I do' ten times. Nothing felt different, but she still thought it was a good idea to do what her father said. He was really wise. *Maybe something will happen later,* thought Sammy.

She twisted and turned and thought about being the ideal football player. She started imagining that she was playing at her very first training for the Shooting Stars. It was the last kick of the game at the end of the session. The teams were tied 3–3. Sammy got tripped up just outside the penalty area. Coach Kev gave her team a free kick and told Sammy to take it. Sammy picked up the ball and put it calmly down on the spot where she had been fouled. She took five steps back, bent down and rubbed the gold comet on the side of her shoes. 'I believe, I do,' she said under her breath. Big breath in. Big breath out. She ran in. WHACK. In slow motion the ball spun its way through the air to the top right-hand corner of the goal. The goalkeeper had no chance. Before she could even celebrate, the players on her team were jumping all over her.

Before Sammy could say any more 'I believe, I dos' she fell asleep. She dreamed she was like Marta at the FIFA

Women's World Cup. Dribbling, around one, two, three, four players, just as if they were stuck in the mud. She even went around one player three times and another player four. The 50,000 people in the stadium were cheering, but she was concentrating so hard that she didn't hear them. But when she kicked the ball over the top of the goalkeeper to score the winning goal, the crowd went wild. The noise was deafening. *One day*, Sammy dreamed, *that could really be me*.

When morning came, reality came with it. Sammy sat up in bed and suddenly knew that dreams don't come true with just some 'I believe, I dos' and a dream-filled night. Sammy had four days before the all-important training session with the Shooting Stars. Four days to train and practise, and try to be the best that she could be. Only four days.

Her alarm clock said 6.30 and she scrambled out of bed, startling Splodge who was curled up asleep in his basket on the floor. He wasn't used to getting up at 6.30 — why was Sammy in such a hurry?

Still curled in his basket, he watched as she looked behind the door, under the bed, beside the cupboard. It was easy to work out what she'd lost.

She'd been so flakey last night, chatting on the phone for hours to her friends, especially Kelly. When she went to bed she'd just floated down the hall and hadn't put anything away. She hadn't even said goodnight to him.

She was muttering to herself now. 'Where did I put the ball last night? Where is it?' Sammy looked everywhere in her room, even dumping the contents out of a cupboard into a pile in the middle of the floor.

Splodge watched her for a while. Suddenly he had an idea. *I know*, he thought. He thumped his bushy tail on the floor, then rushed into the sitting room and over to the sofa. Crouching down, he wriggled his way underneath, and disappeared completely.

'What on earth are you doing, Splodge?' asked a very puzzled and still-sleepy Sammy. Three muffled barks answered her from under the sofa. *Well, he must be OK*, she thought. *Splodge only barks three times when he is excited. Or he wants to do something.*

Now she was even more curious. Sammy got down on her hands and knees, and turned around. She leaned down and peered under the sofa. All she could see was a mass of black and white spots, but it certainly wasn't Splodge. It was a big black-and-white spotty ball.

Behind it was Splodge trying to push it out with his nose. He wasn't having any luck. The ball seemed to be stuck fast.

'Thank you, Splodge,' Sammy murmured. 'How did you know I left it there?' She reached in, put her arms around the ball and pulled. It still didn't come.

'OK,' said Sammy. 'We need to do this together. I'll pull and you push with your nose. On three. One, two, three — go.'

Sammy pulled and Splodge pushed as hard as they could. A minute passed. Sammy's face started to go red, and Splodge's nose looked all squashed.

They had just about given up, when suddenly the ball came free. Sammy went flying over backwards. She didn't drop the ball, though. When she stopped rolling, she was hard up against the TV, and she hugged the ball to her chest and giggled. Splodge barked.

'Shhh. Mustn't wake Mum and Dad.'

Splodge crawled out from under the sofa. He wagged his tail and put his paw on top of the ball.

'Look,' Sammy exclaimed. 'The ball matches your paws. In fact, it matches all of you! Both of you are white and covered in black patches. Except that the ball has nice neat round spots and you look as if someone has dripped splatters of black paint on you.'

Sammy gave him a good pat. 'But you know I think you're the cutest dog in the whole world, and you're the smartest. Let's go up to the park and play football. I've only got five days to become as good as I can be. But first I have to get some things from my room.'

Splodge answered her with three more woofs. Then he ran around madly in circles. 'You silly dog, you'll make yourself completely dizzy. Stop chasing your tail. Why don't you bring the ball to my room?'

Sammy got up from the floor and rolled the ball to Splodge, who stopped it with his right paw. Just like a professional footballer, he started to dribble the ball. There was one big difference, however: Splodge was using his nose.

When Sammy walked into her bedroom, Splodge was already sitting next to her bed. His paw was on top of the ball again.

'I can't believe how fast you are at dribbling. You're amazing. I hope one day I can dribble that well.'

Sammy walked over to her wardrobe and opened the

doors. She reached up to the top shelf where the night before she had remembered to put her brand-new Comet shoes. Her parents had given them to her last week for her ninth birthday. They were bright pink with gold comets on the sides. Underneath the shoes were lots of smallish bumps. Her dad said they were to help stop her slipping over on the field. The bumps were mostly pink like her shoes, but the tips were gold, like the comets. The bumps and the colours on the shoes made them really stand out.

Sammy took her Comet shoes down from the shelf. She put them under one arm while she felt around for some football socks. The first pair she picked up had purple and green stripes. She showed them to Splodge. He lay down and put his paws over his eyes. 'I guess you're right,' Sammy laughed. 'They won't go very well with pink and gold shoes. I'll look like a fashion disaster. What about these ones?' she asked as she held up a pair of long, white socks with a gold band around the top.

Sammy got the three woofs she wanted. She quickly put on her shoes and socks. When she was finished, she looked at herself in the mirror. Her knobbly little knees peeped out between her baggy shorts and the tops of her socks. Her new shoes made her feet look like flippers. They looked huge compared with the rest of her.

While Sammy was dressing, Splodge started to nose the ball in front of him. He wanted to dribble it out the door.

'Wait, we have to tell Mum where we're going. Sit down for 10 seconds.'

Splodge did what he was told. His tail was still twitching with excitement and his ears were pricked up. He was ready to go. Finally, after half a minute, Sammy ran past him and out of the bedroom door. She stopped when she reached the hallway and looked around for a moment. 'Mum,' she whispered. 'Where are you?'

Sammy's mum didn't answer, so Sammy went looking for her. She wasn't in her bedroom. After searching for a while, Sammy went through the kitchen to the back of the house.

Through the sliding glass door Sammy could see her, sitting on her special sunflower seat.

It wasn't a real seat, it was a ledge that stuck out from the big rock wall leading up to the Banks's flower garden. Sitting on the seat, Sammy's mum looked as if she was floating in a sea of sunflowers. You couldn't really see the ledge, just a person surrounded by a lot of sunflowers. Mrs Banks loved to sit there with her cup of coffee in the early morning. At that time of year it was the best spot in the garden to watch the sunrise.

Mrs Banks waved to Sammy through the glass. Sammy opened the sliding door. When she poked her head through, her mum said, 'Hi, Sammy Banks. What are you up for, so early in the morning?'

'Splodge and I would like to go to the park to have a kick around, and practise for the trials. I want to try out my new Comet shoes some more. Is that OK?' Sammy asked. Then she added, in a hurry, 'I have to practise and before school is the only time. It's light now. I'll be back in time to get ready for school.'

'And have your breakfast,' said her mum.

'Yes, promise.'

'I'll walk down with you. I'd like to see how your new Comet shoes work out. Just let me change my slippers.'

'Thanks, Mum,' Sammy said. 'We won't be too long.'

Sammy found Splodge already sitting at the front door waiting to go. The early-morning sun was on his fur and his tail was thumping up and down on the floor. The big spotty ball was next to him. 'Good boy for being so patient,' Sammy said to him. 'Mum's coming, too.'

'Ready,' said Mrs Banks as she came into the hall. 'We can go now.'

Splodge let out an excited bark. An early-morning run was unusual for him. Sammy swung open the front door. To her surprise, Splodge jumped over the ball with his front two paws. At the same time he grabbed the ball between his back paws. Then he flicked the ball up so that it went sailing over the top of the two of them. It went out the door and landed on the deck right in front of them. The flick he'd just done was exactly like the one Renee had showed Sammy the day before. Well, not exactly the same. He was using four legs, not two.

'Wow, Splodge. How on earth did you learn that so quickly?' Sammy couldn't believe what she saw. 'I want to be able to do that as good as you. Quick, let's go to the park to practise.'

Splodge stood with his head cocked. He still couldn't believe his luck.

'Come on!' said Sammy. 'Let's practise for the Shooting Stars.'

Sammy scooped the ball up as her mother joined them. The three of them walked across the brown wooden deck to the steps and then down onto the concrete path. The left side of the path was lined with trees, and because it was summer they all had the yummiest fruit hanging on them. There were plums, apples, oranges, and grapefruits. Most of all, though, Sammy loved the oranges. Even now, she wanted to stop and pick one. They looked so round and juicy, she reached out to pick one.

"Why don't you wait and have one with your breakfast?' suggested her mother. 'It will taste even nicer then.'

At the top of the path, at the end of their garden, Sammy stopped.

'Which way shall we go to the park? Sammy said to her mother. 'Run up the steps or go the long way around the rock terraces?'

Before Mrs Banks could reply, Splodge raced around the corner of the fence. He was heading up to the steps between Sammy's house and the three huge rock terraces next to them.

'Splodge, wait. You forgot something.' Sammy put the big spotty ball down on the path. She took a step back, and gave it a good kick. It went flying through the air towards Splodge. He had picked a perfect spot to stop just in front of the steps. The ball bounced once. When it came down for the second bounce, Splodge caught it perfectly. Right on the end of his shiny black nose. He turned around and carefully continued. With the ball still on his nose, he went up all of the 99 steps, one step at a time.

Mrs Banks laughed. 'I think you've got some competition, Sammy!'

They caught up with Splodge just as he got to the top. He flicked the ball up in the air for Sammy to catch. 'You really are the smartest dog,' Sammy said. She gave him a big pat with her free hand. He wagged his tail even faster.

The gate to the park was 50 metres from the top of the steps. 'Race you to the gate!' yelled Sammy. She took off as fast as she could. Splodge was much faster than Sammy, so he waited, counting to five. Then he raced after her. Within 20 metres he'd caught up with Sammy, and he barked as he whizzed past her. When she got through the gate, he was already sitting calmly in front of the old red-brick clubhouse, licking his paws. Sammy was huffing and puffing.

'OK. You win, Splodge smarty-pants,' said Sammy, still puffing loudly. 'One day I'll catch you. Then it will be you puffing away like me.' She puffed some more. 'I reckon in five days I'll be faster than you, so there.'

Sammy looked around the park which sat above the three rock terraces. Because it was high up above the rest of the town, it got the very first rays of the sun. Today everything was tinted with a pinkish glow as the new day's sun sat clear of the horizon. Sammy's shadow stretched right across the park, almost to the clubhouse, where her mother was sitting in the sun, watching.

To the left side of the clubhouse, there was a big wire fence to stop balls going down onto the road below. Through it, you could see just about the whole of the town of Eden. Everything sparkled.

Sammy looked across at the apartments, three storeys high, that lined two sides of the park. Sammy looked up at Coach Kev's apartment window. It was closed and the curtains were drawn shut. *Good*, she thought. She wasn't going to kick a ball anywhere near his place this morning.

Sammy looked in the other direction, into the sun. It was hard to see anything because of the glare, but she could see a few other people running around the field, training. She squinted into the sun and watched. Suddenly her own efforts seemed hopeless. These people were really serious about their sport. Sammy was just a kid having fun with a dog.

She felt all her confidence drain away. She wasn't a football player. All she'd done was accidentally kick a ball into Coach Kev's custard. She was nothing, really. She started to walk back towards her mother, then she heard someone shout, 'Sam-meeee!'

It was Renee, her boots swinging over her shoulder.

'Hi, Renee.'

'Great to see you! We can kick to each other.'

And suddenly Sammy felt a bit better.

'How did it go yesterday after I left?' asked Renee.

'Too much to tell you.'

'Try me — but you'd better be quick. I need to do some training. I'm going to the United States in a few weeks on a football scholarship. I need to work hard!'

'Wow!'

Sammy told Renee about the ball and the custard. Renee roared with laughter. But when Sammy told her about Coach Kev's offer, Renee stopped laughing. 'Hey. That is so ace! Good on you!' She clapped Sammy on the back. 'You'll be part of my old team!'

Sammy smiled, but then a niggle of doubt crept back in. All the teams in her town had mostly boys. She'd heard that when the girls wanted to play, the boys were sometimes really mean.

Sammy asked, a little shyly, 'Is it true that when the girls want to play, the boys on the team can be mean?'

Renee took the question seriously. 'Let me tell you about when I joined the Cougars.'

Sammy nodded. The Cougars were good, but they were the most unpopular team in the league. They were also the Shooting Stars' biggest rivals.

Renee told Sammy that when she arrived for training on her first day, the team was very unfriendly. No one talked to her. They didn't want anyone to take their place, Renee said. 'Especially not a girl.'

That was why they tackled her extra hard. They pushed her and pulled her long hair, but that wasn't the worst. The worst was what happened after the training.

'Like what? What happened?' asked Sammy.

'You wouldn't want to know.'

'I would!'

Renee started putting her boots on. She didn't look at Sammy while she talked.

'The Cougars had just finished on the field. They were having their bottles of orange juice or water that they'd been told to bring from home. I'd forgotten to bring mine so I didn't have anything to drink. Don't you forget your water bottle, for training.'

'No, I won't,' said Sammy.

'One of the quiet boys, Fred, said he'd get me some orange juice from the club. He went out of the changing room. He was gone for a while, but eventually he came back with a cup of orange for me.'

'Nice,' said Sammy.

Renee tied her boot lace very tightly. 'I was really thirsty. I swigged down the whole cup in about five seconds flat. Just before I swallowed the last gulp, I realized that something in my mouth was wiggling. And it was slimy. I spat what was in my mouth back into the cup. In the cup I saw two big fat worms. I was nearly sick right there and then. I ran off the field and never went back.'

'That's terrible.' Sammy shuddered.

Renee went on to tell her that the Cougars coach had called her to say that the team was sorry. He said they weren't normally so badly behaved and Fred had been stood down from playing as a punishment. For putting worms in her drink, he wasn't allowed to play for two weeks.

The coach also told Renee that the players had thought she was good. They just wanted to test her, he said, to see whether she was really tough. If she went back, he would make sure it never happened again.

'Despite the coach's apologies, I wasn't convinced. I was so angry at them all for laughing, and especially that jerk Fred. The Cougars coach pleaded and pleaded, but I wouldn't budge.'

'So?'

'I'll never play for the Cougars.' Then Renee tossed back her long hair and laughed. 'I am totally over that now. And I got into the Shooting Stars, which is a better team than the Cougars will ever be! And look at me now! I have a scholarship to go to the United States.'

Sammy stared at her, impressed by Renee's spirit.

'See, if you want something bad you never give up,' said Renee. 'Come on! Let's practise!'

Sammy threw the ball and they both ran after it. She had no intention of sneaking off back home now.

Every day for four days Sammy got up half an hour earlier than normal and went to the park with her mum and Splodge. Every day for those four days, Sammy practised on the field as the sun rose in the sky. One day it rained, but still she practised as her mum watched from under her umbrella. Nothing was going to stop Sammy getting better and better at kicking and dribbling, and gradually she built up her fitness by running around and around the field.

Sometimes she saw Renee, but not always. Some days she was good at kicking. Some days she wasn't so good. Some days those niggling doubts came back again.

'If I actually get into the team,' she said to her mother on the third day, after running up the steps, 'what if they really hate me. They're nearly all boys. They might even make me drink worms like those other boys did to Renee. Maybe I shouldn't even go to try out.'

While Splodge stood a couple of steps higher up than she did, with his head cocked to one side, her mother quietly said, 'And what about that secret weapon your father told you about?'

Sammy thought for a minute and then grinned. She gathered her confidence together and got rid of the niggling doubts by saying out loud 'I believe, I do' 10 times quickly. Then she breathed deeply. In, then out.

On the third morning, she worried about not being good enough.

'What if they don't want me in the team?'

Splodge just stood there, waiting, panting, with a little smile. This time her mother reminded her about what Renee had said, and how she went hard-out for what she wanted. And they continued up the steps to the field.

Her mother made delicious dinners. Her father took his time saying goodnight to her every night. On the third night, he told her about how he had been a swimmer when he was young and he'd had to get up even earlier, every day, to train in the pool which was a long car ride away.

'I didn't know you were a swimmer, Dad.'

'No? Well, when summer comes, we'll go to the beach and I'll teach you to surf.'

'Yes, please!'

'Go to sleep now. Tomorrow is the day you get to try out for the Shooting Stars.'

'I know. I won't be able to sleep at all.'

'You will.' He switched the light out and softly walked out of the room.

Within seconds Sammy was fast asleep, dreaming her dream about playing football with Marta.

The next morning Sammy woke up with a start. The sun was just beginning to shine in the window and onto Sammy's bed. Sammy pulled the covers back, and put her feet on the floor. She felt butterflies in her stomach, and her arms and legs felt tingly.

She rushed into her parents' room. 'Wake up! Today's the day!'

Her mother was already up. She was in the kitchen making a big breakfast.

'Pancakes! Yum!' shouted Sammy.

'Try to calm down,' said her mum. 'You have the whole day to wait before you go to the Shooting Stars training.'

Her mother told her to get her things ready for school.

Rushing around, Sammy grabbed all the things she needed from her room. Comet shoes first. They were the most important. Into her schoolbag they went with her homework. On top, she threw her favourite Soccer Babe t-shirt, black football shorts, and socks.

'You'd better put in something warm for after training,' her mum said. In went her shiny black tracksuit.

There wasn't much room left in Sammy's schoolbag. Her lunch and drink bottle would have to go in a plastic bag. She tied that onto the schoolbag. The big spotty ball would go under her arm.

'Right,' said her mum. 'Get yourself ready now.'

It took Sammy a record 10 minutes to get herself ready. Uniform on, teeth brushed, and hair put up into her normal snork, Sammy went into the kitchen to show her mother she was ready. The pancakes were sitting on a big plate in the middle of the table. Suddenly she didn't really feel like them this morning. Her tummy felt like it was in knots. But she had a big day in front of her. And pancakes, dripping with maple syrup, were the best food ever.

She had seen someone on TV saying that the best foot-ballers ate really good breakfasts. Your body was a bit like a car. If you didn't put petrol in a car, it stopped. Same thing if you put the wrong petrol in. So she knew that if she played football and didn't have the right breakfast, she would just putter out on the field. No breakfast meant no energy to keep up with the others. Sammy didn't want that. She needed all the help she could get today. A footballer's breakfast was definitely essential.

She looked at the pancakes again. 'Sorry, Mum, I think I'm too nervous for pancakes.'

'That's fine. Those are for your dad. He's decided he's going to start his swimming training again, after work today. I'll make your usual.'

After some cereal with fruit, and then eggs with toast, Sammy was ready and raring to go. She gave her mum a kiss goodbye and headed out the door to school.

When Sammy arrived at Eden Park Primary School, there was no one there. All her friends were probably still at home, just starting to eat their breakfast. It didn't matter. Sammy wanted to kick the ball against the big concrete volley board. She wanted to get in some practice before the big trial that afternoon.

Sammy took off her black leather school shoes and slipped on her Comet boots. Standing a foot or so away from the wall, she passed the ball to the wall. Back and forth, hundreds of times, just as if she had a friend there to kick with. If she did a good pass, then the ball came straight back. If she did a bad one, she would have to run after the rebound. So it was a good idea to concentrate, otherwise Sammy got really tired running after the ball.

When Sammy had done 20 passes without a mistake, she moved two steps back. It got harder and harder not to kick the ball in the wrong place. It was fun, though, and pretty soon she was sweating from all the hard work.

After she'd been kicking the ball against the wall for 30 minutes, she heard a voice behind her say, 'Hello Sammy. What are you doing here so early?'

Sammy turned around to see Ms Hope, the coolest teacher in town. She had long black dreadlocks and tiny square black glasses. The best thing was that she played football. Sammy's mum said the newspapers and TV said she was the best adult player in the country, even including the men. Sammy thought that was something special.

'Coach Kev asked me to train with the Shooting Stars today after school,' she told Ms Hope. 'I wanted to practise because I don't want to be bad.'

'That's great news, Sammy. Really great news. But it's not about being bad. Think about it differently. It's about wanting to do your best. And you should want to do your best. Even being asked to try out for the Shooting Stars is a great honour. You should be very proud already. Coach Kev wouldn't ask you along if he didn't think you have something special.'

'I don't think it's specialness I've got,' said Sammy. Then she told Ms Hope about the football in the custard.

Ms Hope laughed, then she became serious. 'That was a lucky break for you. It's up to you now to show that you do have that special stuff. Give it everything you've got. Don't hide it away because you're scared of looking bad. Take your chance to shine like a real shooting star.

'Once I had to go to a trial for the national team. I was scared just like you. There were players there who had been playing in the team for 10 years. They were much older than me, and some of them were better players. At first none of them talked to me because I was new. Maybe they thought I was going to take their place. I was so nervous I nearly threw up.'

Sammy couldn't believe Ms Hope would ever have been that nervous. 'What did you do? How did you get over it?'

'What I did was I just focused on little things. I watched the ball. I marked my player. I ran as much as I could. I did the simple things. Instead of trying to do a fancy long pass, I did a short one to the player nearby. All those sorts of things.

And it worked. When I got the simple things right, I felt more relaxed. Then I could start trying harder things, like dribbling and tricks.'

'Do you think I should do that, too, Ms Hope?'

'Definitely, Sammy. Let me know tomorrow how you went. I'd like to know. Is that OK?'

'Yes, Ms Hope. Should I come to your classroom at morning tea time?'

'That would be great, Sammy. OK, I think it's time for you to put your school shoes on. The bell will go soon. Good luck this afternoon, Sammy. I am sure you'll do fine. You looked pretty impressive at the volley board just now.'

Ms Hope patted her on the shoulder and walked over to the school gate. All the girls and boys were arriving for school. Amongst them was Kelly, who had been Sammy's very best friend for three years. When she saw Sammy sitting on the ground putting her shoes on, Kelly rushed over to her.

'Oh my god, Sammy,' shrieked Kelly. 'I don't believe it. I've just heard the most a-mazing news!'

'You never told me you were going to try out for the Shooting Stars! Kane, the right back, is one of my brother's friends and he told us on the way to school. And you'll never believe what he said.' Kelly's voice rose into a shriek.

'What did he say, Kelly? Tell me quickly,' said Sammy, pulling at the sleeve of her friend's uniform. 'And how does he know anything about it?'

'He said that the Shooting Stars had a pre-training talk last night. All the players from last year were there. Coach Kev told them you would be trying out for the team today. Is that true?' Kelly asked. 'Is it really, really true?'

'Yes, it is.'

Kelly danced around, yelling, 'Ace! Ace! Ace!' then she stopped, spun round and said, 'Tell me everything. Totally everything.'

Sammy told her the whole story from start to finish, including the football in the custard. 'I bet Coach Kev didn't tell the team *that* bit of the story,' she said.

They grabbed hold of each other, they were laughing so much.

Sammy told her about the practising, and about Renee.

'She is so cool,' said Kelly.

'Dad rang Coach Kev to say I was allowed to play. I have to go to the Shooting Stars' club today after school. Training starts at 4 p.m.'

Kelly was still looking happy, but Sammy knew her well enough to notice she was also holding something back.

'What else?' she asked.

'Oh, nothing,' said Kelly. She looked down at the ground.

'What's wrong? Is there something else?'

'I shouldn't tell you . . . but, well . . . Kane said the team didn't want any more girls. They already have two. But they like them because they're really good and score lots of goals. And he said they didn't want someone who hadn't played before. And he said you look so girly you'd be a dumb player.'

It was Sammy's turn to look at the ground. She felt as if someone had just kicked her in the stomach. She forced herself to think about Renee. She wasn't going to let a wimp like Kane get in her way. She was silent so long, just looking at the ground, that Kelly was worried.

'Don't worry, Sammy. Kane is just nasty. He hasn't even seen you play. I'm sure the others won't be like him.' Kelly put her arm around her friend. She had to reach up a bit, because Kelly wasn't very tall for nine years old. 'You'll show them, no problems.'

'I will, too,' said Sammy, and they high-fived.

Normally, Sammy loved school. PE was by far her favourite subject because she got to try different sports. She also enjoyed Social Studies and Science. This morning, though, school went really slowly. Every minute seemed like an hour.

The first class was Geography. Mr Lucas was the teacher. The boys and girls in Sammy's class all thought he was strange. He had a long beard that used to be black but was now mostly grey. He always wore blue shorts and grey socks. That wasn't so bad, but to top it all off he wore roman sandals. Kelly whispered to Sammy that he must have got dressed in the dark. It started them laughing all over again.

Mr Lucas talked about Switzerland. He said something about mountains and cheese, and — well, Sammy didn't know what he was saying because she stared out the window and thought about football. Vaguely she heard Mr Lucas mentioning fondue, which was a national food of the Swiss. It was made of hot, melted cheese and looked a bit like custard.

Custard! Suddenly Sammy jerked back from her football daydream. Sammy didn't dare look at Kelly. Then she just couldn't help it, and let out a tiny giggle. Kelly started giggling, too.

Mr Lucas stared across at the two of them. 'You're being very silly this morning, Sammy. Anything wrong?'

'Sorry, Mr Lucas.'

Sammy felt bad and decided she'd have to be sensible and be in control of herself to get through the day. She thought about her football heros. She didn't think they would have giggled through classes.

Mr Lucas asked her a question, 'So what would you put in? Sammy, what about you?'

Because Sammy hadn't been listening to Mr Lucas's speech about Switzerland and fondue and mountains, she hadn't got a clue what he meant. He was asking what you would put in a fondue, but all she had heard was 'custard'. She thought the question might have something to do with what had happened with Coach Kev.

I'd better tell the truth, she thought. *Mr Lucas must know about the ball in the custard.*

'What's the answer, Sammy?'

'The ball,' she said.

The class burst out laughing. Kelly laughed the most.

'What ball? In the fondue? That wouldn't be too tasty. Do you think bread might be better?' Mr Lucas asked and looked down his nose at her.

'Yes, Mr Lucas. It would.' Sammy was very embarrassed.

'Might be a good idea to concentrate, Sammy Banks. You'll find the time goes a lot faster, and you might just learn something!'

Sammy took Mr Lucas's advice. For the rest of the morning, she listened to what the teachers were saying. Time did go faster when she wasn't daydreaming and the teachers were a lot nicer.

At lunchtime, she ran out to the field to have lunch with Kelly. 'What have you got today, Smelly Kelly?' That was her pet name for Kelly, but only she was allowed to say it. If anyone else did, there would be trouble.

'Marmite, cream cheese and walnut sandwiches,' Kelly replied. 'What have you got?'

'Peanut butter and banana sandwiches. Want to go halves?'

'No way. They sound revolting.'

'They're not. They taste really good. And Mum said that they'll give me lots of energy for this afternoon.'

'Well, you'd better eat them then. How are you feeling? Excited?'

'Yes and no. I . . .' Sammy didn't get any further.

Kane suddenly appeared in front of them with four other boys and one girl. They closed in on where Sammy and Kelly were sitting.

'There she is,' Kane sneered. 'The one who thinks she can

play football. She thinks she can be a Shooting Star. What a joke.' He kicked Sammy's lunchbox and one of the peanut butter and banana sandwiches fell onto the grass. 'Ewww, look at that. She even eats baby mush.'

'Yeah, what a joke. They don't let babies play in the Shooting Stars. You'll never get in, so don't even bother trying,' said one of the other boys, who had blond, spikey hair. His name was Nick.

'Go back home to your dolls, Sammy,' said the only girl in the group. She had long black hair tied up in a red ribbon. Her name was Josephine and she was in their class. They knew she did ballet and was always Miss Goody-good in class.

Sammy looked so angry Kelly thought she might burst. Or, worse, hit out at Kane, or kick Josephine. If that happened, Sammy could end up with a detention and then she wouldn't be able to try out for the Shooting Stars. Kelly jumped between them.

'You should be ashamed of yourself,' she said to Josephine. 'Does Sammy say anything about you running around in a silly frilly dress and slippers all the time? No, she doesn't. So don't be mean to her.'

Sammy picked up her sandwich. Kelly thought Sammy might plaster it over Josephine's face, so she held her friend's hand down.

Kelly turned to the boys, 'As for the rest of you, you're just a bunch of stupid idiots. You haven't even seen her play. When you do, you'll be sorry for what you said. You'll see.'

Even though Kelly was tiny, the others backed away. She stood there, with her hands on her hips, staring at them. 'So, what are you hanging around for?'

Kelly was waiting for an answer, her eyes blazing with anger. They kept backing away, then they turned and sauntered off, trying hard to look cool.

Kelly packed her lunchbox and shoved it in her bag. She picked up Sammy's and put her lunch away, too, then grabbed Sammy by the arm and marched her to the other side of the field. Sammy's anger seemed to have disappeared. What was left was nervousness. She didn't look at Kelly.

'Please don't listen to them, Sammy,' Kelly said.

'But maybe they're right. Maybe I won't be good enough,' Sammy answered.

'That's not true. They're just trying to put you off. Kane's probably worried that you'll be better than him and the others are just jealous. Coach Kev asked you to try out for the Shooting Stars, not them. Please believe me. It's true.'

'Sometimes I wish I'd never kicked that ball through his window!' mumbled Sammy.

25

For the rest of the day, Sammy was very quiet. She didn't talk about the Shooting Stars but concentrated on her schoolwork, as Mr Lucas had told her to. Kelly watched her, worried. When the bell rang for the end of school, Sammy just gave Kelly a wave and said, 'See you tomorrow.'

Kelly looked at her friend. 'Hey, are you OK?' she asked.

'Yep,' said Sammy.

'Not nervous? Excited?' asked Kelly.

'Nah,' said Sammy, pretending to yawn, pretending to be very bored with everything. 'No big deal.'

The acting was so good that Kelly thought it was for real. She thought Sammy might not care whether she became a Shooting Star or not.

'I'll walk with you to the ground,' Kelly said.

'No, it's OK.'

Kelly narrowed her eyes. 'I'm coming whether you like it or not.'

Sammy smiled. 'I'm not giving up if that's what you're worried about. I am serious about going to the stadium,' she said. 'Let's go.'

She tucked her spotty ball under one arm and linked her other arm with Kelly's. They walked past the long row of old wooden houses next to the school. While they were walking, Kelly chattered away. Sammy just listened. She didn't feel like talking, she didn't want to think about anything that would take her mind off playing her best. She didn't want to see things or hear things. Instead, Sammy wanted to find that one deep place inside that was her own sense of herself and what she could do. She just wanted to concentrate — she was getting prepared.

At the end of the street, Sammy and Kelly stopped to cross the road. The house facing them on the other side was really old. It was also very run-down. Bits of white paint were peeling off the sides of the house. Tiles were missing from the red roof. One of the front windows was broken and had a big cross taped on it.

When they had made it safely to the other side of the road, they saw two children playing on the driveway of the run-down house. One was a boy and the other a girl, both about seven years old. They were shouting and laughing, obviously having lots of fun. Sammy and Kelly went to look closer. The children were playing football, but not with a real ball, just a large, round ball of string. They were kicking it barefoot. They didn't seem to care, even though the hard ground must have been hurting their feet.

'Where are your shoes?' Kelly called out to them.

The children stopped playing and looked towards the girls. It was obvious they were twins. They both had red hair, very white skin and big freckles dotted all over their faces.

After a while, the little girl answered shyly, 'We don't have shoes for football. We only have two pairs and we aren't allowed to get them dirty.'

'Doesn't kicking hurt your feet?' Kelly asked again.

'We're used to it. It only really hurts if you stub your toe,' the little girl told her. She was wearing shorts and a green sweatshirt that was three sizes too big for her. The sleeves were flopping over her hands.

'Why don't you go to the park and play on the grass?' asked Sammy. 'Then you won't hurt your feet so much.'

The young boy spoke for the first time. 'The other kids will tease us because we haven't got a proper ball.'

'Oh,' said Sammy, feeling the spotty ball under her arm. She thought about Kane and his horrible teasing. Being teased was something no kid liked. 'Do you like playing football?'

The two children's faces brightened up suddenly. 'We love it, we love playing football. It's the best. It's so much fun,' they shouted together.

'I want to be a Shooting Star one day,' the little girl said. 'I dream about it every night. But I don't think they let girls play.'

'Actually they do,' Kelly told her. 'There are two girls in the team. And guess what? Sammy here is going over there right now to try out.'

'Wow. How cool is that! You must be a really good player. They're the best!' the boy said with his mouth open wide.

Kelly grinned at him. 'She's really good. Maybe you could come and see her play one day for the Shooting Stars.'

'That would be awesome,' his sister answered. They now had huge smiles on their faces.

'Hang on,' said Sammy. 'I'm only trying out. I might not get in.'

'Of course you will!' said Kelly. The twins both smiled at Sammy and nodded.

'What are your names?' Kelly asked.

'I'm Red,' said the boy. 'And she's Ginger. She's my sister.'

'OK then, Red and Ginger, we have to go. Sammy's got something important to do.' Kelly beamed at her friend.

'Bye, kids. We gotta go.'

The Shooting Stars' stadium was across another small road to the right of Red and Ginger's house. It wasn't really a stadium as far as football stadiums go. There wasn't room for 80,000 or even 20,000 people singing in the stands, like some of the football games Sammy had seen on TV. Instead, there was only a small stand at one side of the pitch nearest the road. Only 200 people could sit there — the rest had to sit on the grass banks around the other sides of the pitch. Everyone in Eden still called it a stadium, though — after all, it was the biggest park in town.

Sammy and Kelly walked across the road and followed the white wooden-board fence that surrounded the stadium. The entrance was at the other end. To get in you had to walk under a huge white archway which said *Welcome to the Shooting Stars* in silver. On top of the arch was a massive yellow star with streaks coming out of it.

Kelly stopped under the archway. 'One Sammy safely delivered to training. Mission accomplished,' she said. 'I have to go home now, but good luck this afternoon. I know you'll be great.'

Kelly gave Sammy a big, hard hug.

'Ow, aah. You'll squash all the air out of me. I won't be able to run at all if you keep that up,' laughed Sammy.

Kelly laughed too. 'See you later. Text me. Tell me all the news.' She waved as she walked back around the fence in the direction of her home.

Sammy took a deep breath. *Here I go*, she thought.

She said out loud, 'I believe, I believe, I believe, I do, I do, I do' and swung in through the impressive gate.

Coach Kev had told Sammy to meet him at 4 p.m. in the changing rooms. There was still 10 minutes to go. She decided to have a look around the clubhouse. It didn't look too different from the houses in the street. The white painted boards just seemed a bit more stretched out. The roof was made of wavy grey corrugated iron. On top was another long sign saying *Shooting Stars*. It had a symbol of a shooting star, matching the one on the archway.

Sammy walked around the path to the front of the club. By the door was a grey cat, curled up like a ball in the sun, and she stopped to stroke the little ball of fluff. The cat purred happily, stretched, and then went back to sleep. *He's got white paws just like Splodge,* Sammy thought.

When she stood up from stroking the cat, she noticed a man standing in the doorway. He was tall and very brown. 'Hello,' he said. 'My name is Mr Nicholls and I'm the cat's caretaker. His name is Socks.'

'Oh,' said Sammy. 'Nice name.'

'Socks is the club's cat. It's his job to keep the rats away, which he's very good at. Every time Socks catches a rat, I give him a big bowl of cream.'

'Lucky cat,' said Sammy.

'I'm also the President of the Shooting Stars. You must be Sammy Banks. You've come to try out for the team. Is that right?'

'Yes, sir,' answered Sammy. 'I have to be in the changing rooms in five minutes.'

'Well, you certainly don't want to be late on your first day. But you have a few seconds. You can walk through the club to the changing rooms. If you go this way, you'll be able to see all the cups the Shooting Stars teams have won.'

Sammy stepped over Socks, in through the clubhouse door, into a large room. At one end of the room was a stage. Behind it was a massive board with lots of names on it.

'That's the honours board. When someone in the club

does something special, we put their name up there — if you get into the national team or you spend many years helping the club. We're very proud of the people up there. They worked very hard to get their names on that board,' explained Mr Nicholls.

Sammy looked at the list of names. At the bottom, newly painted in blue, was Renee's name. She gasped.

'Do you know Renee?' asked Mr Nicholls. 'She's a role model for us all. She's worked very hard to get where she is now.'

Then he pointed to the other side of the room. The whole wall was covered in trophies on glass shelves. Some were just about as big as Sammy. Others were round plates. Sammy had never seen so many glittering prizes before.

'That is also a wall of honour,' Mr Nicholls went on to say. 'You see, Sammy, when you play for the Shooting Stars you don't just play for yourself, or even for your team. You also play for all the people who have worn the shirt before you and all those who play after you in years to come. If you play for the Shooting Stars, you must wear the shirt with pride and honour. It's a big responsibility.'

Sammy listened to what he was saying. *It's incredible how much the Shooting Stars mean to so many people,* she thought. *From Red and Ginger, to people who have been dead for many years.*

I really do have to try hard this afternoon, she told herself firmly.

After showing her some of the gleaming trophies up close, Mr Nicholls led Sammy through to the changing rooms. There were four — two for visiting teams and two for the home team. Mr Nicholls knocked on the door of the changing room with *Number One* on it.

'Coach Kev,' he said, 'I have Sammy out here. Would you like her to come in?'

'Yes, please,' was Coach Kev's answer.

Coach Kev held the door open for Sammy to walk through. When she followed him in, she saw 16 pairs of eyes on her. 'Hi, there. This is Sammy, everyone,' he said. 'Please take a seat, Sammy.'

Sammy glanced quickly around the room. The benches in front of the lockers were all full except for one space, the one next to Kane. As Sammy walked over towards it, she could feel everyone staring at her, especially Kane. It made her feel nervous. Sammy didn't look at anyone. She put her schoolbag and spotty ball in an empty locker and sat straight down. She leaned slightly away from Kane.

Kane leaned over towards her. 'What are you doing here? I thought you understood. You aren't meant to be here,' he whispered fiercely in her ear.

Before she could answer, Coach Kev started talking. 'Welcome to the last training before the season starts, everyone. Good to see you all — and Sammy, a special welcome to you. I hope you enjoy training today.

'We want to make this year as good as the last one. That means we train today as we mean to play. No slacking around because it's not a match day. I want to see 100 per cent effort from everyone.' All the players nodded.

'Good. So what I would like to do today is this. Rob, you take the warm-up to start with since you'll be the captain again this year.'

'Yes, sure,' answered a strong-sounding voice in the corner. Sammy looked up at Rob. He looked as tall and strong as he sounded. His face looked as though he lived an outdoors life. It was all healthy and glowing, and his eyes were really shining.

Rob will be my friend, Sammy thought. Just as she did, he smiled at her. It was as if he knew. It seemed as though he was already her friend.

'Thanks, Rob.' Coach Kev continued with his plans. 'After the warm-up, we'll play some fun stuff to get you puffing a bit. Then we'll do some skill work and small-sided games.

We'll finish off with a game — eight vs eight. Does that sound good?'

'Yes,' said a chorus of voices. Sammy's wasn't one of them. *Eight vs eight? Small-sided games? What does that mean? What on earth is Coach Kev talking about?* she thought.

Coach Kev pulled Sammy aside as she walked through to the girls' changing room. 'I know you won't understand everything I say just yet. Don't worry, that's normal. It takes a while to learn all the new words. If you don't know something, don't be afraid to ask me. Or ask one of the players. They all know what it's like being new. They had to do it once, too, you know.'

Coach Kev went on, 'The other thing you can do if you don't know what to do, is to step out of the session and watch for a while. If you see things a couple of times before trying them, it will be a lot easier. OK then? Off you go. Put your gear on and we'll see you out on the field.'

Everyone except Sammy had come to the ground in their football gear. She had to change out of her uniform into the gear she had brought. The others were already out on the field kicking the ball around. She had to hurry.

Sammy quickly changed into her Soccer Babe shirt, shorts, and football socks. Then last, but most important of all, she put on her Comet shoes. Before she put them on, she rubbed the sides of them. 'I believe, I do,' she said and took a big, deep breath. Sammy slipped her boots on and ran out of the changing rooms onto the field.

The team had just started their warm-up. 'In twos,' Rob yelled out. Everyone paired off. Sammy was at the back with Silvia, one of the best players in the team. It didn't seem to matter that she was a girl: people said she was so good because she'd played in a boy's team in Germany. Her mum and dad were from there, and she'd lived in a place called Munich until she was eight years old. Sammy had heard that they were really good at football in Germany. Their grown-up women's team had even been world champions, just like their men's team.

Silvia still spoke with a German accent. 'Ve go?' she said when it was their turn to start running. Off they went, jogging around the marked-out field in two lines. Coach Kev had put cones around the top right-hand quarter of the football pitch. The team had to run around the outside of the cones. Rob was running alongside the team in their pairs. They jogged once around the cones slowly.

This is OK, Sammy thought. *I can do this.*

After the first lap, Rob started to yell out orders. 'Right, everyone. Listen carefully. You have to concentrate. When I say up, it means down. You have to bend down and touch the grass. If I yell down, you have to jump up. As if you are heading the ball. Cross means change places with the person next to you. If I say backwards, you turn and keep running in the same direction but backwards. Forwards means you stop and run forwards again. Left means run to the right. Right means run to the left. Think and move. Got that?'

Sammy couldn't believe her ears. So many instructions. She went through all the things again in her head. *Down is up, up is down, cross is . . .*

'Left,' she heard suddenly. Everyone went right. Sammy was still thinking. She banged straight into the person in front. Kane, of all people.

'Good one,' Kane snapped at her.

'Sorry,' she said.

'Don't worry about him,' Silvia said. 'Keep going. And pay attention.'

'Lucky for you, Sammy, first one is free. Next person to go the wrong way does five star jumps. Same if you're last,' Rob told the team.

They kept running. Sammy was concentrating hard now. *Just do the opposite*, she was saying to herself.

'Down,' Rob shouted.

Sammy jumped. She headed an imaginary ball. She got it right, but she was still slower than the others.

'OK, Sammy, down for five,' Rob told her.

Sammy stepped out of the line. For a moment she didn't know what to do. Luckily for her, Rob saw her confusion. He stopped running, and showed her what to do. Crouching down, he then leapt into the air with his arms and legs in the shape of a star.

Jumping jacks, Sammy thought. *Easy peasy.* Five were no problem for her. She did them all the time at school. Back to the line she ran as fast as she could. They were all the way around the other side of the pitch when she got there. She was puffing quite loudly.

'Not fit, Sammy?' sneered Kane at her.

Right at the moment he said it, Rob yelled his next order: 'Backwards.'

Kane was too busy being nasty to Sammy to hear. CRASH, he went into the player in front of him. The player he bumped into was Hamish, the centre-back. He was a big, strong boy. Kane, who was small and skinny, just bounced off him and fell on the grass. The team all laughed at the funny sight. Sammy laughed too, especially when Kane had to do the five star jumps.

The warm-up went for four more laps around the mini field. The longer they went, the quicker the players got at doing things. Sammy kept focusing hard on what Rob was telling them to do. She also improved. Only once more did she have to do star jumps.

When Coach Kev whistled, Rob brought the team to a stop by the goal in front of the clubhouse. 'Have a drink and a stretch,' Coach Kev said to them. The players picked up their bottles from behind the goal. Sammy had left hers in the changing room.

'Do you want to share some of mine, Sammy?' asked Hamish when he saw she had no drink with her. He had a nice, smiley face. He certainly wasn't worried about what happened with Kane.

'Thanks, Hamish. I'm really thirsty,' she answered and went to take the bottle from him.

'Sammy,' interrupted Coach Kev. 'I would much prefer you got your bottle from the changing room. Haven't you heard about the dangers of sharing spit, even if it is just on a drink bottle? I know there's nothing wrong with Hamish, but it's always better to not make exceptions to a rule. Agreed?'

'Yes, Coach Kev,' replied Sammy. 'Can I go get my drink bottle then?' He nodded his head.

By the time Sammy returned, the players had started stretching. They were using the metal pipe fence that went around the field to lean against. Like the others, Silvia was pushing the bar with both hands. Her right leg was straight behind her with her heel on the ground. The left leg was in front, but also with the foot flat on the ground. They all looked like they were trying to push the fence over.

'What are you doing?' Sammy questioned Silvia.

'Ve are stretching our calf muscles,' she answered.

Sammy was confused. Little cow muscles? Where were they?

'This von here,' Silvia continued. She pointed to the muscle at the back of her leg, under her knee, the opposite side from her shin.

Sammy copied what the others were doing. She felt a big stretch at the bottom of her leg. *It works*, she thought. *I can really feel that.* It was the same for all the other stretches they did. Foot straight up in front on the bar. Bending one leg behind and holding the foot, other hand holding the bar. Lunging with one foot out in front holding the bar. With each exercise, she felt different areas of her body get warmer. It felt really good, especially afterwards. Sammy stamped both feet in her new Comet shoes. She was now ready to run around again.

31

'Right, that's enough,' said Coach Kev after they had been stretching for 10 minutes. 'Time to get going. Into groups of four, everyone. We're going to do some relay races.' He numbered the players one, two, three, or four. 'Line up behind the cones. Ones closest to me. Fours at the other end. Last one there goes down for 10 press-ups.'

The players sprinted for the line. Luckily, Sammy was closest to the line so she wasn't going to be the last one. Kane had been picking the grass out of his boots and throwing it at the goalkeeper, Frank. He didn't hear what Coach Kev said. Kane started running well after the others.

'The last one to make it — that's you, Kane,' announced Coach Kev.

Kane had to do the press-ups. He mumbled that it wasn't fair because he hadn't heard. Coach Kev took no notice. Kane still had to do the press-ups. No one in the team watched him.

When they were in their groups of four behind the line, Coach Kev told them what they had to do. 'Everyone in the team goes once,' he said. 'Each time through gets points, and the team with the most at the end is the winner. Winning team gets to tell the losers what they have to do. Any cheating or pulling out, you get points taken off. First time through is a simple sprint to the cone, touch it, turn around and sprint back. No ball. Easy. Ready, steady, go.'

Sammy's team got out to a good start. Rob was first out and he was in first place when he came back and tagged Sammy. She was running second. Sammy was fast, but Sasha, the other girl in the team, was also running second. She was even faster than Sammy. In fact, Sasha was the fastest in the whole team. Sammy got to the end first, but by the time she turned and reached the finish line Sasha had overtaken her.

They had two more to go, though. Hamish was one and Silvia the other. Hamish pulled back the lead against Sasha's team and it was all down to Silvia. Silvia started really well. She even reached the halfway turn-around first, but right on the finish line the boy who played on the wing for the team just snuck in front of her. He had quite long hair for a boy and he was short. His name was Lionel.

'Great run, Lionel,' said Coach Kev. 'Four points to your team. Three to Rob's. Two to Sasha's. And Kane, your team gets one point. Better pick your game up or you'll be running around the pitch. Or worse!'

Kane dug his boot into the grass and didn't look at anyone.

'Next race,' Coach Kev went on to say. 'This time it's just a straight dribble to the end cone and back. Out with the right foot and back with the left. Go.'

Funnily enough, exactly the same thing happened. The teams finished in exactly the same order. Rob put Sammy's team in front early on. Sammy did well to hold her own against Sasha with the ball.

Thank goodness I did all that practice this week, Sammy thought. Then she banished all thoughts and just concentrated on the ball beside her foot.

'Good one!' Rob said to her when she tumbled back over the line.

They were still in front after Hamish had his turn. It came down to Lionel versus Silvia as to who would win. Lionel was even more speedy with the ball than he was without it. He pipped them again, right on the line.

The next time around it was different. They had to dribble around the five cones in the middle of the start and end cones. The cones were one metre apart. Lionel and Sasha's team came last this time. Their team went too fast. Twice they had to go fetch the ball when they lost control dribbling around the cones. The same happened to Kane's team, who were also well behind after chasing the ball across the field.

Sammy's team did well, but again they didn't win. The four players in the team that did were all attackers. They played either in midfield or up front. Matu, from her class, was one of them. He played on the right wing normally, in front of Silvia. Her position was right midfield.

'So they should win that race,' Rob said to Sammy and their two team-mates. 'It's their job to do the tricky stuff. But we are doing very well. We're performing consistently. Not up and down like the others. If we keep this up, we'll win. We're on nine points with Sasha's team. The attackers are on eight. We're all in the race still. Kane's team is out already. They've only got four points.'

'Last one,' announced Coach Kev. 'This time you have to juggle the ball out to the first cone, dribble between the cones, and juggle to the end. Then dribble straight back. You can pick the ball up to help you get started juggling. Got that?'

A look of panic came across Sammy's face. She didn't know how to juggle the ball yet. Oh, no!

Sammy tugged Rob's shirt. 'Rob, I can't do this one,' she told him.

'Why not? Is something wrong?' He looked concerned.

'No, I can't do juggling. I've never tried before,' Sammy answered.

'How do you know if you've never tried? Just give it a go. Some of the others aren't that good either. It might not be as bad as you think. I know what, why don't you go last? The three of us are quite good at juggling. We can try and put the team in front so at least you have a head start.'

'OK,' she said, but she wasn't so sure.

She waited for her turn, trying to be brave.

As Rob promised, he, Hamish, and Silvia put the team out to a good lead. It was Sammy's turn. She stopped the ball with her foot when Silvia dribbled it back to the line. Picking it up with her hands, Sammy dropped the ball down to her foot to start juggling. It bounced straight back up. *So far, so good*, she thought. The next one, too, she managed to bounce off the top of her foot to make it go straight up. The third one, however, was a disaster. Sammy's foot was floppy so the ball just ran off the side. Worst of all, it went across the path of the other teams. She had to run around the back of them to get it. Then she had to go back to where she was and start again.

By the time Sammy returned with the ball, all the other teams were finished. Everyone was watching her. The ball dropped four times on the ground before she was able to get back to the line. Sammy felt really embarrassed.

'Good try, Sammy,' Rob said when she finally finished. He patted her on the back. 'It's not that easy when you start.'

'She needs to practise vith the ball, Rob,' Silvia said to him. 'It's not good enough.'

'Sorry Silvia, I did try,' Sammy protested.

'It's OK, Sammy. You have to start somewhere,' Rob said as he turned to Silvia. 'Give her a chance will you? Not everyone starts juggling at the age of two like you.'

'Sammy needs to know vat she needs to do to get better. And do it. Otherwise she von't get in the team,' Silvia explained. 'I vill help . . .'

Silvia had to stop. Coach Kev was starting to talk, and no one talked when he was talking. 'Good effort, you lot. I've worked out the points and it was close. Last on eight points was your team, Kane. You'll have the pleasure of doing what the winners decide for you. Third was Rob's team on 10. And we have a tie for first. Sasha and Matu, your teams got 11 points each. Well done. You can decide what the losing team has to do. You've got one minute. The rest of you get a drink.'

The two winning teams huddled together. They had lots of ideas about what to make Kane's team do — Lionel wanted to make them run around the field five times after training. David, who usually played left midfield for the team, said they should do 10 sprints to the halfway line. Someone else suggested they should pick up chewing gum off the ground for half an hour.

Matu thought carefully about the ideas. 'They're all good suggestions,' he said. 'But let's think about this. What happens if we're the losing team next week and Kane's team wins? Will the ideas be so good then?'

Coach Kev called them in. 'What's the decision, Sasha?' he asked when the rest of the team had finished their drinks.

'We thought of a lot of things for them to do. Cleaning toilets was a favourite. Sprints to halfway was another,' Sasha teased. Kane and his friends were panicking. 'In the end, though, we didn't want to be too mean. It is the start of the season, after all. All you have to do is take the nets down from the goalposts after training.'

Kane and his team sighed with relief. It was nowhere near as bad as they were expecting.

'That's good for me, too, Sasha. Good decision,' Coach Kev said. 'That's that then. On to the next exercise. Stay in your teams of four. We're going to play some small-sided games. Two groups of four against four. Rob, you take your team over to the grid in the corner. Put the red bibs on. Kane, your team can play in yellow against them. The other two teams, you are in the grid next to it. Matu, your team put on blue bibs. Sasha, your team the orange ones.'

Sammy followed her team-mates over to an area in the corner. It was marked out by cones, and she guessed it was about 15 metres by 15 metres. That must be the grid Coach Kev is talking about, she realized.

She also realized they weren't putting babies' bibs on. *Thank goodness*, she thought. The bibs were brightly coloured vests that helped you see who was on your team.

But what was a small-sided game? Sammy looked around for help. She didn't know what to do.

As Rob handed Sammy her red bib, he took her aside. 'Small-sided games are just like a real football game, just with fewer people on each side. Plus you have a smaller pitch. That means you get lots of touches of the ball. But it also means you have to do things quicker. Do you think you can handle that?'

'Yep,' Sammy responded. She was looking forward to actually playing football.

Sammy moved into their grid with the others. Coach Kev gave some more instructions: 'Ball is out if it goes outside of the cones. If the last kick came off your team, the other team kicks it to play in from the ground. No throw-ins. To score a goal, you have to dribble between the two cones one metre apart on the opposite goal line. All as clear as mud?' He smiled at them. No one said anything. 'OK then. Red and yellows, you're off,' he said.

He threw the ball into Sammy's team's grid. She could hardly believe it. She was actually playing a game with players from the Shooting Stars.

Coach Kev had thrown the ball right over to the far right-hand side of the grid. All the players had been standing on the left side listening to Coach Kev. To start with, they all stood like candlesticks. The players just looked at the ball. Suddenly, Silvia moved. She ran towards the ball. 'Quick, ve have started. Don't stand like statues.' Everyone sprang into action. The game had begun.

Silvia got to the ball well before the players on Kane's team and dribbled the ball straight towards the cones. She was only a metre away when Mark came flying over. He was used to tackling. Mark played right at the back in the middle of the team with Hamish. Often he had to save the team from goals being scored against them. This time, Silvia was about to dribble into the goal. He slid in front of her. Luckily for his team, the ball went into him, not the goal. The ball bounced out of play.

Normally it would have been a corner kick. The ball had come off Mark. The rules in this game were no corners, so Mark took a goal kick from between the cones. He meant to pass it to Kane who was calling for it on the right-hand line of the grid. The ball spun off his foot slightly. It went to Sammy. This was her chance!

'I believe, I do,' she whispered. She trapped the ball perfectly and started to move forward. Two seconds later, she was lying on the grass. Kane had run in from the wing and pretended to tackle her, but he had pushed her in the back instead.

Coach Kev stopped the game. 'Free kick to Reds.'

Rob brought the ball back to where Kane had fouled Sammy. 'You take it, Sammy.'

Sammy got up off the ground and straight back into the game. She passed the ball quickly to Hamish, who was standing up front. No one was near him. All of the other team had run forward to help Kane. They were still running back. Hamish dribbled the ball easily through the goal. 'One nil, we're brill!' Hamish shouted with a big smile on his face. He ran back to behind halfway of the grid with his arms stretched out like an airplane, just like the professional footballers on TV. Hamish high-fived Sammy. 'Great pass,' he said to her.

'That was just a fluke,' Kane piped up. He kicked the ball off again. The Yellows managed to keep the ball amongst themselves for five passes. Kane had the ball again. The easiest thing for him to do was to pass to Mark, who was in the clear to his right. No one was marking him. But Kane wanted to be fancy instead and dribble past Sammy. Just then, he kicked the ball a bit too far in front of him. She took the ball off him, pushed it to the right, and ran around him.

Kane didn't like Sammy beating him at all. As Sammy followed the ball past him, he stuck his knee out. It caught her right in the thigh. She was knocked off balance. Down went Sammy again. This time it hurt. Sammy stayed there. She couldn't move.

Sammy held her leg where Kane had hit her.

Coach Kev ran onto the pitch. 'Are you OK, Sammy?' he asked her. 'Where does it hurt?'

Sammy didn't answer. Coach Kev asked again, 'On your leg where his knee got you?'

Sammy nodded. She couldn't speak because she was trying hard not to cry.

'I think it's best you take a break. Let's take you over to the side and put some ice on your leg. Can you get up?' Sammy slowly got to her feet. She took a step forward on her sore leg. Her leg felt quite numb.

'Help me take Sammy to the seats by the clubhouse,' Coach Kev said to Rob.

'Sure thing,' he answered. Facing each other, Coach Kev and Rob bent down on to one knee. They crossed their arms over and joined hands, making a seat for Sammy to sit on.

'There you go, Sammy. Your own special *arm*chair!' Coach Kev laughed at his joke. 'It's a seat fit for a football queen. Put your skinny arms around our necks and jump on up.'

Sammy sat herself back into the human chair. She was only light. The two of them lifted her up, no problems. They carried her to the front of the clubhouse and carefully put her down on the wooden bench.

'Keep your sore leg up,' said Coach Kev. 'I'll go get some ice. Rob, you start the game again. Tell Kane he gets to sit out for that tackle. That makes it fair. Three versus three.'

Kane moaned his head off when Rob told him he could not play. But there was nothing he could do. He sat on the side and sulked.

36

Coach Kev brought an ice pack wrapped in a tea towel back from the clubrooms. He had a quick look at her leg. 'It'll be right. You'll just have a bit of a bruise tomorrow. Nothing to worry about. When you're ready, come back and join in. We'll be playing a full game soon.'

From the bench, Sammy watched the others playing for a while. They looked as if they were having so much fun. The players were running all over the place, shouting and making lots of noise. When someone scored, they jumped up and down. And they often jumped on the goal scorer.

She held the ice pack to the bruise. Slowly the pain faded. Part of Sammy wanted to go back out there, but the other part of her was too scared. She didn't want to get hurt again, and she didn't want Kane to be mean to her again. And she didn't want to look silly again because it was all new to her, like when they did the juggling. Or because she didn't know what something meant. She had started after the others and they were too good for her now. She felt miserable, and she began to feel as if she didn't belong.

Home, that's where she wanted to be, with Splodge, in front of the TV. She didn't want to be here, sitting on this bench, in the cold. Sammy decided to get up and go home.

Now. She could at least tell her parents that she tried out with the Shooting Stars. She'd tried, and she wasn't too bad, but she didn't want to be in the team, even if they offered her a place, which they wouldn't. She was sure of that.

Sammy took the ice pack off her leg and put it down beside her. She stroked Socks, who had come up and bunted her hand with his nose. Picking herself up off the bench carefully, she put all her weight on her right leg, the good leg. Then slowly she tried her weight on her left leg, which felt better after the ice but was still a bit stiff.

I'll go and find Mr Nicholls, she thought. *He can ring my parents and ask them to come and get me.*

Just as she went to walk away, Sammy saw two little faces peer around the corner of the clubhouse. It was Red and Ginger. They broke into huge smiles when they saw her, and rushed over to where she was standing.

'Hi Sammy,' they said together.

'Hi. What are you two doing here?' Sammy asked. Her voice was flat.

'Mum said we could come over to watch you.'

'Why aren't you playing with your team?' asked Ginger.

'I hurt my leg,' she replied. 'It feels a bit better now, so I'm going home.'

'Why are you going home if it feels better?' Now it was Red's turn to ask questions.

'Because . . .' Sammy couldn't think of a reason. She couldn't tell them she just didn't want to try any more. They had come to the field especially to watch her.

'Because why, Sammy?'

'Because they have enough good players already. They don't need me,' Sammy told the twins. Their little faces looked so sad, Sammy looked away from them. 'Look, sorry you guys, but I have to go home. See you later.'

With that, Sammy hobbled past them to the changing room to get her things. Then she was going home.

The twins watched Sammy walk around the side of the changing rooms. As she disappeared into the building they could tell by the way her shoulders were hunched that she wasn't happy.

Even though Ginger was only seven, what Sammy had said didn't seem right. She said to Red, 'If they had enough players, why did they ask Sammy to train with them? And her friend said she was really good, so why couldn't they just put her in the team?'

Before Red could answer, a ball flew over and bounced near them and Rob came running after it. It bounced a couple more times before it finally stopped rolling right in front of the twins.

Rob was surprised to see them there. They were his next-door neighbours. Normally they weren't allowed to play in the park.

'Gidday, you two. What are you doing here?' Rob asked.

'We came to see Sammy play but she went home,' Ginger explained.

'Was her leg hurting?' Rob wanted to know.

'A little bit, but it was better. She said she was going home because the team didn't need her. She thought you had enough players,' Ginger told him.

'Oh no! Where did she go, Ginger? Quick, tell me. Perhaps I can get her back before Coach Kev sees she's gone.' Rob picked up the ball and kicked it back to the field.

Ginger pointed to the changing rooms. 'In there. She was going to get her things first.'

'Thanks, Ginger. I'll be back soon.'

Rob rushed off towards the changing rooms. He wasn't allowed to go through the club and had to go around the path. No walking inside with boots on was a strict rule at the Shooting Stars club. Anyone who did had to clean out the changing rooms for a week. It wasn't a nice job. It took forever to pick up the grass, used tape, banana skins and bottles from the games at the weekend.

Rob opened the door to the four changing rooms. 'Sammy, are you still here?' he called out.

No answer.

Drat, Rob said to himself. I must have missed her. What am I going to tell Coach Kev? He'll never let her come back again.

Just as Rob turned to go back out the door, Sammy appeared in the hallway. She had gathered up her things and had her bag in her hand, but hadn't changed out of her football gear.

'Sammy! Thank goodness. The twins told me you were going home,' he said, sounding worried.

'I am,' she answered.

'Why? Is your leg bad?'

'It's a bit sore, but that's not the reason I'm going home. I'm not good enough to be here. That's why Kane keeps kicking me.'

'Kane doesn't kick you because he thinks you're bad. He kicks you because he thinks you're good,' Rob said.

'What? That's crazy!'

'It's true! Even though he's been playing the longest, he's

nowhere near being one of the top players. Every time a new player comes along, he's scared they'll take his place, especially when they're as good as you. That's why he's nasty. He thinks it will put the new ones off. Most of the time it does, and they don't come back. It's a real shame. Some of the players he's scared off could have been really good. At the same time, they didn't pass the test. So maybe it's a good thing they left.'

'What test are you talking about, Rob? I don't understand.'

'Some of the teams we play against have players like Kane. In fact, the Cougars are all like Kane. They pick on weak players. They shout at their own team-mates. They play unfairly. Sometimes they even try to hurt other players.'

Rob sat down on a bench and Sammy, still hunched over, sat beside him.

Rob continued. 'They do that because they can't beat you playing football. They have to do other things to win, just like Kane is doing to you today. If you leave now, it means you would do exactly the same in a real game. Walking away isn't the sign of a champion. Champions stick with it, even when things are tough.'

Sammy shook her head sadly. Her snork waggled from side to side. What Rob said was a different way of looking at it. She had to think again. It was a hard thing to do.

The sign of a champion? Yes, she was beginning to understand what he meant. No champion would walk away from Kane.

'Kane is a test for you, Sammy, and you have to pass it. Instead of walking away, think of how you should deal with him. Be smart, use your brain, and don't just accept it.'

'That's what Dad would say.'

'Sammy, I know because Kane did the same thing to me when I started. I was a bit luckier because I was bigger than him. He couldn't hurt me physically, but he was real mean to me. I also wanted to give up. But in the end, I wanted to play football. I wasn't going to let some nasty dork stop me.'

That made sense to Sammy. She looked at Rob. 'I want to play football, too,' she said.

'Good. Football is bigger than Kane.'

'I guess so,' she said. 'But how do I—'

'You don't win against Kane by running off home! I stuck it out. Now Kane wouldn't dare try anything against me.'

Sammy sat there, her legs swinging back and forth. She didn't know what to do now: go home or stay here. Just how brave was she? After all, Rob was much bigger than she was. It would have been easier for him to put Kane in his place.

Rob waited for her to make up her mind. He didn't push any more. The decision had to be hers.

Finally, she asked, 'What did you do to change him?'

'Do you really want to know?'

'Yes. Please tell me, Rob.'

'OK.' He leaned over and whispered in her ear. One minute later Sammy was laughing her head off.

It had happened two years before when Rob started playing. Kane had been horrible to him right from the start. One week at training, Kane had called Rob useless in front of everyone. Rob had tried to ignore him but Kane got worse. The more it went on, the more Rob got annoyed. Ignoring Kane wasn't helping, so Rob decided he needed to do something.

The perfect opportunity came in the fourth game. They were playing away at another team's ground. It had been raining all week and the field was covered in massive puddles. There was mud everywhere. By half-time, everyone was covered in it. They were sticky brown from head to toe.

Normally the team stayed on the field for half-time. That day, the weather was so yucky that they decided to go into the changing room. Luckily, Coach Kev had also thought ahead. He knew it would be muddy so he'd brought a second strip with him. When they got to the changing room, Coach Kev told them to take a new strip out of the kit bag. But don't take the shorts on the top, he had told them. They needed to be stitched again.

Rob was nearest to the bag so he took out the shorts that needed to be repaired. He got his new strip and went back to his place along the bench where his water bottle was. Rob changed into it quickly. It felt much better to be warm again.

In the meantime, Kane had got his strip too. He didn't change into it straight away. Kane wanted to go to the toilet so he put the strip down on his seat, next to Rob's.

When Kane was out of the room and everyone was busy changing, Rob quickly swapped Kane's good shorts with the ones still in his hand, the ones that needed repairing. He put Kane's back in the bag. By the time Kane got back, everyone was starting to go back to the field. He was in such a hurry to change that he didn't notice the shorts were falling apart.

Within 10 minutes, the whole team was covered in mud again and their strips were heavy with all the extra weight. It wasn't long before Rob could see holes appearing in Kane's shorts.

Give it 10 minutes, Rob thought.

It was actually less than that. The opposition striker had got a breakaway. Kane was the only one left in defence who could catch him. He sprinted across the field from right back and did a huge slide tackle. The striker saw Kane coming and stopped the ball on the spot. Because it was slippery, Kane couldn't stop. He went sliding past the striker and the ball. Kane ended up on the other side of the field — completely without shorts. They got left behind in a puddle.

At first Kane didn't know he'd lost his shorts. He was very wet and muddy and he didn't feel anything was missing at all. So Kane kept running around. For five whole minutes, he ran around in his undies. It wasn't until the people on the sideline started laughing that he realized something was wrong. Finally, the ball went out. Rob, who had picked Kane's shorts up out of the puddle, waved them around. He yelled out so everyone could hear, 'Are these yours, Kane?'

'From that point on, he left me alone,' Rob said to Sammy. 'It was my way of standing up for myself. I didn't have to use my fists. And I didn't walk away. Sammy, you shouldn't either.'

Sammy laughed again. She was feeling so much better. That awful feeling of not belonging had gone. And her leg didn't seem so bad, either.

'You're right, Rob. Why should I let someone like Kane stop me from reaching my dream? I love football. I want to play for the Shooting Stars. I need to pass the "Kane" test. And I think I know just how I'm going to do it.'

'How?' He stared straight at her, smiling. He raised his eyebrows, waiting for her answer.

'To start with, I am going back on the field to finish training.'

'Go you, Sammy!' Rob said. He gave her snork a little pull. 'Come on. We'd better get back. Coach Kev will wonder where we've gone. You can't just disappear from his kind of coaching session.'

Sammy left her things where they were in the changing room. She and Rob ran back down the path to the field. She was limping a bit, but she was determined to play. The teams were just finishing up the small-sided games.

'Nice of you both to join us,' Coach Kev said with a twinkle in his eye. 'Couldn't you find the ball, Rob?'

'Sammy needed some help with her leg,' muttered Rob. He didn't want to say what had really happened, knowing Coach Kev wouldn't be pleased if he knew Sammy had wanted to go home.

'How is it, Sammy? Are you up to playing a game?' Coach Kev asked her.

'It's fine, Coach Kev. I'm up to a game. Just try and stop me,' Sammy answered, even though her leg was still hurting. She wasn't going to let anyone see, though, and especially not Kane.

Coach Kev looked surprised. The look on Kane's face was even more surprised.

Coach Kev was quiet for a moment before he said, 'Great, Sammy. Your team is going with the Oranges. You need to change your bibs. Blues and Yellows go together and wear blue. We're going to play across half of the pitch. Oranges, you attack the goal nearest the street. Rob, you organize your team into positions. Matu, you organize your lot.'

Once everyone had the right bibs on, Sammy's team went out on the pitch. 'There are eight of us,' said Rob. 'They've got Frank, so we'll have to play rush goalie. Hamish, you can do that and play in the middle at the back. Andres, you go in your normal position on the left beside him. Michael, you slot in at right back. In the midfield, I'll go in the middle. Lionel, you go on the left in front of Andres. Silvia, on the right. Sasha and Sammy, you'll be our strike force. I think you should play more on the left, Sammy — against Kane. Right everyone, let's get lined up then.'

The players set themselves up in their positions. Sammy's team had the kick-off. Coach Kev gave them the go-ahead. Sammy passed the ball to Sasha to start the game, and ran straight up into the forward line.

'Kane,' Sammy said when she stopped level with him. 'You're about to find out why I'm here.' She looked him straight in the eye.

After Sasha received the ball from Sammy, she passed it back to Rob. Rob pushed forward from the midfield with the ball. He looked up for someone to pass to. Immediately Rob saw Sammy coming towards him. She had just turned away from Kane and was now calling for the ball. Rob side-footed a perfect pass to her feet.

It's up to me now, Sammy thought. *Look out, Kane.*

Before she trapped the ball, Sammy looked quickly behind her. No one there. She turned the ball neatly with the inside of her right foot. She dribbled as fast as she could at Kane. He came up to tackle her at full pace. Kane wanted to tackle her really hard. *Scare her a bit again*, he thought.

He was heading straight for her right foot. Sammy saw he was going too fast to change direction. Kane had lifted his foot as far as he could backwards to make a huge tackle on her. Quickly she moved the ball across her to the left.

Thank you for the lessons, Splodge and Renee! she thought.

Kane's foot swung forward into thin air. He'd put all his weight into the tackle. As a result, he went flying through the air behind his leg, landing with a big plop on his bottom.

One—nil to me, thought Sammy. *Yeah!*

She dribbled straight for the goal. Frank the goalkeeper came rushing out to challenge her. Meanwhile Sasha had sprinted up to help. She was calling for the ball to her right. Just as Frank dived, Sammy slipped the ball to Sasha. The goal was empty. Sasha had oodles of time and dribbled the ball up to the goal line. Just before it, she stood with one foot on the ball. None of the defenders had run after her. So she just waited there until Mark finally came. When he was about a metre away, she calmly back-heeled it into the goal.

'Grrrr,' Mark said to Sasha. 'That was cheeky.'

She didn't care. Sasha was already running over to high-five Sammy.

'Top stuff, Sammy girl,' she shouted. 'What a great start! Let's do the victory dance.' Sammy had no idea what 'the victory dance' was. She watched Sasha doing her thing for a few moments. Sammy laughed as she copied her. They looked like they were stirring butter with their arms and shoulders.

'That's enough, you two,' Coach Kev stopped them. 'Get back to your side of the field for kick-off.'

Sammy had forgotten all about her bruised leg. She flew back across the field, passing a miserable-looking Kane on the way. She gave him her sweetest smile.

The two teams battled it out for 20 more minutes. Everyone was trying really hard. They all wanted to be in the team for Saturday. It was always great to play in the first game of the season. It meant you were a first-choice player — at least to start with.

Matu's team scored the next two goals. The first one started when Sammy tried to pass a ball back to Rob. He was running full-speed from the midfield. Unfortunately, Sammy passed a bit behind him and Rob over-ran the ball. It went straight to David's feet. When the quiet blond boy turned, all he saw was space in front of him. All Rob's team was up in line with him. Like Sasha, he had a clear run to the goal.

The second goal was completely different. It was a goal-mouth scrap, more like a game of pinball than football. Taye, who'd only joined the Shooting Stars at the end of last season, took a corner. The ball landed right in the middle of the goal mouth. It bounced once. Matu half-volleyed it with the top of his shoelaces. The ball hit Silvia's leg and cannoned off her straight into the goalpost. It bounced back into the middle of the goal mouth again. By now no one could see the ball because everyone was around it. They were either trying to kick it out of the goal or kick it in.

Jordan, who was normally a substitute for the Shooting Stars, whacked it really hard this time. It ricocheted off Hamish's knee, shot up in the air, and bounced off Matu's head. Then it went sailing into the top right-hand corner of the goal. It was a bit lucky, but it was a goal.

'That's what counts,' Coach Kev said afterwards. 'Doesn't matter how it goes in.'

It took Sammy's team five minutes to make the score even again. Again she played a big part in setting up the goal. The ball had bounced free on the left side of halfway. Sammy and Kane were both five metres away on opposite sides of the ball. Sammy saw again that Kane was coming in as hard as he could. She rose to the challenge.

I'm going to win this, thought Sammy.

They were going to reach the ball at the same time. Dribbling around him wasn't an option. Sammy had to make herself as strong as she could. She didn't back off. She flew in and block-tackled him, bringing one foot in after the other against the ball.

Kane, on the other hand, tried to kick at the ball as hard as he could. Despite Sammy being five kilos lighter, Kane bounced off her. She stood firm, like a brick wall, while he fell over. Once again, she had put him on his bum.

No time to celebrate this time. As soon as Sammy had won the ball, she layed it off to Lionel. He was running into the middle from the left. Lionel was very tricky. He dribbled around the last player which was Mark, then Frank the goalkeeper, before passing the ball into the net.

Lionel's goal made the score 2–2. 'Last goal is the winner,' announced Coach Kev. 'Let's see who's got it when it counts.'

After Coach Kev's announcement, the game got faster. It also got scrappier. Both teams desperately wanted to win and they weren't giving anything up. End-to-end the ball went for seven more minutes.

Sammy had been standing out on the left wing. Kane was marking her closely. Suddenly the ball came flying over the top of them. Both turned and raced for the ball. It was 10 metres away, not far from the left-hand side of the goal. Sammy and Kane sprinted as hard as they could. Their faces were straining. Neither wanted to lose.

When they got to the ball, Sammy touched it first. She pushed it in front slightly. Kane, instead of running alongside, ran across her — catching her right on her sore leg. She went down, rolling once before she came to rest on her stomach. Sammy didn't move.

The players on both teams gasped. The tackle looked really bad. For a moment no one moved. They didn't do anything. It was Coach Kev who finally got into action. He ran over to her from the other sideline.

'Sammy are you OK?' he asked. All he could see was her snork hanging over her face. He tried to make a joke, 'You get 10 out of 10 for that dive. That was super spectacular!'

Underneath all the hair, Sammy was scrunching her face. Her leg was hurting. But worse for her was the fact that she had let Kane get her again. She was mad with him, and madder with herself.

I am going to show him once and for all, she vowed.

Sammy blew the snork out of her face. She lifted up her head and said, 'I'm fine, Coach Kev. Can I take the free kick?'

Coach Kev was relieved, but a little surprised by her forcefulness. 'Absolutely, Sammy. Be my guest. You earned it.'

Coach Kev picked the ball up. He rubbed it around a couple of times on his shirt. Then he placed it carefully on the best spot on the grass. 'Top right-hand corner,' he said, and winked at her. As he walked off the field, all of the players in her team were rushing forward to set up for the kick. They all wanted to score the winning goal.

Sammy took a deep breath and got up from the field. She looked over at Rob. He nodded. Then she took a few long, slow breaths. In. Out. She shut her eyes just for a second and said *I believe, I do* deep inside her own head and heart.

She took five steps back from the ball and took another breath. Out of the corner of her eye she saw something small and black and white and shaggy way over on the other side of the field. She snapped back to fully concentrating on the ball, then the goal mouth, then the top right-hand corner of the goal.

I believe, I do, she said to herself. *I believe, I do*. She rubbed the comet on her boot. She imagined kicking the perfect goal.

What happened next was all good. Sammy kicked the ball hard and true. It sailed over the crowd of players in the goal mouth. The ball went straight into the top right-hand corner. Just as Coach Kev had suggested. Just as she had imagined

before she kicked the ball. Just like her dream last night.

Her team erupted. 'Yayyyyy!' they all yelled together. 'We won, we won!'

They ran over to Sammy. Some patted her, some hugged her, and the others just jumped on her. Pretty soon she was at the bottom of a big pile of players. She was a bit squashed, but she didn't care. This was the coolest feeling ever.

Coach Kev stopped the celebrations after a few minutes. 'Time for a warm-down,' he said. 'Two slow laps around the pitch you just played on. Five to 10 minutes of good stretching, then you're done. And that's not stretching your mouths either, you lot. I'll meet you in the clubhouse after that.'

The players went off and did as Coach Kev told them. For the two laps Sammy felt as if she was floating. She was so happy. Everyone was talking about her goal. As she jogged around the end of the field, beside Rob, she noticed Splodge and her father standing, watching. Splodge was on a lead. He was trying to pull Sammy's dad across the field. But Sammy's dad wasn't having any of that. He just stood there, quietly watching, and enjoying Sammy's special moment. She waved at him. He waved back.

When they had finished their stretching, Sammy walked with the others up to the clubhouse. Red and Ginger were still there, sitting on the seat out the front where Sammy had been icing her leg when she had been thinking of going home.

'Sammy, that was the best goal,' Red yelled out to her.

'You're really, really tops,' Ginger added.

'Thanks, you two,' Sammy said back to the twins. Suddenly she had an idea. 'Wait there for a second,' Sammy told them. She ran around the path in the direction of the changing rooms.

A minute later, Sammy appeared holding her big spotty ball. She went over to the twins. 'I want you to have this,' Sammy said as she handed the ball to Ginger. 'You can practise with it until you're old enough to play for the Shooting Stars.'

'Wow, Sammy. Thank you. Can we really have it?' Red said, not quite believing her.

'Yes, of course. But you have to practise as much as you can. Is that a deal?' Sammy replied.

'That's easy. We like playing football. Thanks so much, Sammy,' Ginger said. She gave Sammy a big hug.

Coach Kev stuck his head out of the door. 'Can you come inside please, Sammy,' he said to her. 'I'm about to start.'

'I have to go now,' Sammy said. 'But hopefully I'll see you

soon. Bye.' She waved goodbye to the twins, took her boots off and went into the clubhouse.

Inside the club, the players were already sitting on chairs around a long table. Coach Kev was at the end standing up.

'There's a spare seat up here, Sammy.' Coach Kev was pointing to the seat right next to where he was standing. She quickly slipped into it.

'OK, now that we're all here I just wanted to say a few words before the game on Saturday. As you all know, we won the league last year. In fact, we won it quite easily in the end. There were only three or four tough games, most of them against the Cougars. What I want you to do for Saturday, though, is to forget that last year ever existed. You are not the champions now. You are at the start line with everyone else. Last year doesn't count at all for this year. It's all gone.

'In saying that, I think we have a very good team this year. Perhaps even better than last year. But that may also be the same for the other teams. They may have new players. They might have got stronger or faster or just better. Who knows? So we have to keep working hard at being the best we can be.

And better. Every time you play, every time you train, keep that in your mind. Your opponents certainly will. And they'll all be out to beat you because you are the champions. They want to prove they are better than you. They will save their best games for you, you can be sure of that. In the end, it will all come down to who works the hardest and learns the most. And to who is prepared to get up and try again when things don't work.'

Coach Kev continued, 'On that note, I want to talk a bit about today. You all did very well at training. It is excellent that you're all trying so hard to get into the team to start on Saturday. I could see that especially in the game at the end. I obviously won't be able to pick everyone, but after today, every one of you could be in the starting line-up. Those of you who aren't, you can consider yourself unlucky. But I know that when you do get your chance, which you will, you'll also do really well.

'On Saturday, our first game is against Wolverston. It will be a tough game. They beat us once last year, remember, so please be ready. Have a good rest before you play in the morning. No riding around on your bikes or skateboards. We're playing at their ground, which is the one with the big wolf face at the gate. Kick-off is at 10 a.m., so be at the ground at 9 a.m. please. Don't forget your strip and your drink bottles. Also something warm to put on after the game.'

Coach Kev wanted to say one more thing. 'Sammy, I would like to thank you especially for coming to training today. I thought you did very well. The goal at the end was a cracker. As you probably know, though, we have lots of players trying out for the team. Many boys and girls want to play for us. That's what happens when you have a good team. Everyone wants to join.

'Normally when new players come along, we make them train for four weeks. Then we decide whether they're good enough to join or not. I have to say, Sammy, in your case that's not going to happen. I am really sorry . . .' Coach Kev stopped talking.

Sammy's face fell. She thought she'd done OK, especially scoring a goal. Even Coach Kev had said it was a cracker. It didn't seem fair.

Coach Kev coughed. He picked up the water next to him and had a sip.

'As I was saying, I am really sorry, Sammy. It really helps to train with a team before you play, but you're not going to get that chance. I want you to join us straightaway and play on Saturday,' he said with a big wide smile on his face.

Except for Kane, who looked furious, the other players cheered. Sammy was so shocked she couldn't do anything.

Coach Kev continued, 'What I liked about what you did today was not your spectacular goal. It was certainly a good one, but not the reason I want you to play for the Shooting Stars. It was the fact that you had a tough start, but you still tried. Then you had a sore leg. You still kept going. That's the sign of someone who will do well. We want people like that in our team. Don't you agree, you lot?'

'Yeah,' the others shouted. Kane looked down at the floor, his face all stony.

'Good von, Sammy,' Silvia added and gave her a clap. The others joined in. Sammy had never felt so happy in her life. She was going to be a Shooting Star.

'So Sammy Banks, can you please come up here. Rob has something to give you,' Coach Kev asked her. He swapped places with Rob who was seated in the chair opposite Sammy. She stood up and moved to where Rob was now standing.

'Sammy, on behalf of the team, I would like to present you with your Shooting Stars strip. We hope that you wear it with pride like the rest of us. Good luck for the season. I really hope you score lots of goals like today. No pressure!' The team laughed.

When they finished laughing, he said, 'Seriously, we're glad that you're joining us and not one of the other teams, because then we'd have to play against you! I hope you enjoy playing for our team, because I think it's going to be a great year.' Rob handed her the strip.

'What do you think of that, Sammy Banks?' asked Coach Kev.

'It's the best thing ever, Coach Kev,' Sammy answered. She was shaking with excitement. 'I can't wait for the first game to come. Bring on Saturday.'

'We can't wait either, Sammy,' Coach Kev said. 'Well done. You deserve it.' Then he added, 'You can all go now. See you all on Saturday. Oh, and Kane, don't forget the nets.'

To be continued in *Way to Play, Sammy!*

Some football skills to learn

Now that you've finished reading, here are some things you can do to be just like me on the football field. In *Sammy Joins the Shooting Stars,* I learn to juggle. You can, too — all you need is a bit of space (not near a window or inside), and of course a ball.

- Start by holding the ball in both hands, dropping it onto your foot, and catching it again. Make sure that when the ball touches the top of your foot (your instep), your foot is firm and in the middle of the ball. If it's floppy or off-centre, the ball will run off to the side.

- Once you can do this comfortably, try juggling the ball twice before you catch it. Then three times, four . . . and so on. If you are having trouble getting past a couple, try letting the ball bounce once on the ground between the juggles.

- Once you can do 10 juggles in a row without dropping the ball, you can also try the same thing with your:
  - other foot (all good players can use both feet)
  - both thighs
  - head.

- When you are happy using all the different parts of your body, you can also have lots of fun mixing it all up, going up and down your body. For example, go three juggles right foot, to three right thigh, to your head for three, and then back down the left side for three each on your thigh and foot. Or one left foot, one right foot, head, one left thigh, one right thigh. You can even throw a shoulder bounce in there if you get really good. Each time you do it, try to do more than the last time without dropping the ball.

- You can practise different ways of flicking the ball up to juggle instead of dropping it out of your hands. To start with, put your foot on top of the ball slightly in front of you, drag the ball back with the sole on to the top of the same foot, flick it upwards and start juggling. When you can do that with both your good foot and your bad foot, try these other ways to get the ball up in the air to juggle:
  - Drag the ball back with your sole on to the top of your opposite foot.
  - Put the ball in front of one foot and place the other foot in front of the ball. Do a quick, short back-heel with the foot in front of the ball, so that it runs up the top of your opposite foot.

- Stand like a penguin with your heels nearly together and your feet pointing out to the sides. Put the ball in the space between your feet. Bring your feet together quickly so that the ball pops into the air.
- Put the ball between your heels and grip it tightly with your ankles. Jump and bring your legs up behind you, still gripping the ball. When your feet are parallel to the ground, let go of the ball so that it flicks up and over your head.

Good luck and have fun!

Yours in football,

Sammy